Baptized in Her Seduction

A CHURCH LOVE AFFAIR

SECOND EDITION

Olivia Shaw-Reel

Baptized in Her Seduction: A Church Love Affair

© 2016-2021 by Olivia Shaw-Reel

Book cover designed by Paris Reel of Reel Designs.

ISBN: 978-1-7360500-7-1

Acknowledgements

To those struggling with an addiction or stronghold
of *any* kind, please be encouraged and know that
you CAN be freed and healed.

Thank you to my family, my church home, and my
awesome readers. Your support means
EVERYTHING to me.

*Please also be prepared for lots of plot twists. If you aren't
into them, this may not be the book for you!*

A Message from the Author

This book contains triggering situations and mentions of sexual content, sexual abuse and violence.

Prologue

Birds chirped happily in the gated community while the wind swept through the leaves of the fully bloomed trees. All was silent in the circle of well-kempt condominiums, including the peacefully sleeping woman whose alarm clock had sounded over an hour ago. If not for the snooze button, she would be up now, preparing coffee and a sweet roll.

"Rain. *Rain!* Wake up, beautiful."

The woman, whose nickname was rolling off the lips of her male companion, stirred awake with a groan. Her hazel eyes narrowed as she yawned, while her morning breath smelled of Tequila and the nacho cheese sauce from the Mexican restaurant the night before. She stretched her naked body, still hidden from view. The satin sheets were wrapped around her in such a way that she looked like she was in a cocoon. It would take some serious maneuvering to be able to wrestle her way out.

Her smooth, sun kissed melanin was warm to the touch and sore from last night's festivities. Thinking of the fun she had, and the hearty laughter that flowed from her throat all night, a smile touched her mouth. Her lips were shapely and still tinted with the dark red lipstick that she wore.

"Did you have a good time?" Capri, her longtime lover, chuckled, and watched as her eyes closed. "Don't go back to sleep on me."

"I'm not," she reassured and yawned again. "I had a really good time. I was just thinking about us dancing and acting a fool. I definitely wasn't expecting you to be so...*skilled.*"

"What? I look like I can't deliver?" Capri asked. He looked half offended and half amused. His chest was bare and covered in tattoos. His biceps were naturally bulging and just last night, they had held down her legs as he made love to her for the 21st time.

As crazy as it sounded, she kept track of whom she gave her body to, and how many times she gave it. Capri was one of her favorite men that she frequented; he was such a gentleman, sweet, and just downright *sexy*. His skin was smooth and blemish-free. He reminded her of the actor Michael Ealy, but just a few shades darker. Capri wore his hair in neatly designed cornrows that were gathered with a rubber band at the back of his head. His eyes, a deep-sea green color, were captivating and warm. He also had gorgeous freckles that were painted along his cheekbones. His mother was white, and his father was black, and clearly, they had made a beautiful son.

Lorraina remembered first meeting him at a pastoral convention and it was like a movie scene, the way their eyes locked. At the time, he was engaged and looking for a church home that would complete him. He wanted a ministry that exuded love and was judgment-free. Lorraina's church was no exception, so he and his fiancée joined under her leadership. That following Saturday, their sexual affairs began, and it had been a constant for the last few years.

"No, not at all," she said and then her brilliant eyes focused on him. The sunlight pouring in from the blinds caused her eyes to sparkle in amusement. "Of course, I know you can deliver. But you pulled out some new tricks, and I wasn't expecting it. That's all."

Capri chuckled cockily. "Had to do it big for your 35th birthday."

"I appreciate you. What time is it anyway?" she asked, before lying back down to try to relax for a few extra minutes.

Thankfully, she was only slightly hung-over, and her headache was not as bad as it normally would have been. Over the weekend, they enjoyed shopping, a stage play, tons of fooling around, half-priced appetizers and bottomless drinks. The pair even club hopped like they were in a committed relationship. Capri touched his finger to his phone, so that it displayed the time. "Quarter to eight."

Lorraina cursed and then apologized while looking up towards the Heavens. It was Sunday, also known as the Sabbath day or God's Day. It was also the *only* day out of the week that she refused to curse.

Hurriedly, she shimmied around in the blankets while Capri looked on and laughed. His nonchalance and leisure movements confused her as she finally found an opening in the blankets for her legs, and then left the warm bed. "You're not coming today?"

"And face my wife after being with you for *two* days? Heeeeck no," he said simply while aiming the remote controller towards the 55-inch television screen. He turned to a golf tournament, and then faced her again. "Just text me when service is almost over, and I'll head back home."

"I won't be able to text. We have that guest speaker coming in, remember? I'm her armor bearer for the day," Lorraina said and stood. She scrambled to the bathroom, where a shower would soon take away her sleepiness and achiness.

"Seriously, you should come. It's going to be a great service."

Capri nodded. "It's always a great service. I just don't want to be bothered with that woman. Go ahead."

"Okay." She shrugged and looked at herself in the mirror. She had bags under her eyes, but it was nothing that a little concealer and powder foundation could not cover up. "Well, if you're gone before I get back, I'll see you at the same time and place next week."

"Alright, baby," he called out to her as she stepped into the warm spray pouring from the rainforest showerhead. She scrubbed her skin and fingered through her hair that she had unintentionally sweated out.

Less than thirty minutes later, she was literally running from her condo. She was so spoiled because of her central air that she did not realize how humid it was outside. The weather was going to do some serious damage to her natural hair. She had just blow-dried and flat ironed it.

Wearing all white except her gold accessories, thin, gold belt, and the gold-tipped high heels, she felt good. Last night was just what the doctor ordered, and her body had gotten the workout it needed. Capri and his animalistic lovemaking had her feeling 21 again, instead of the ripe age of 35.

Her white dress skimmed the tops of her oiled knees and was probably a little too tight for her liking. Either she had gained a couple of pounds since the last time she wore it, or the dress had somehow shrunk. She chose the latter option and unlocked the door to her cream-colored 2013 BMW

X5. Clearly, light colors were her favorite, as she settled in the beige, leather seats.

As she drove at a reasonable speed, she slipped on her chocolate-colored shades, and said the short and simple prayer that she always prayed following a sinful night.

"Lord, forgive me for my transgressions."

Then, pulling into The McCall Worship Center, several minutes later, she blew out a deep breath and tried to calm her nerves. As if she was not built for the job, she always grew nervous when entering into the house of the Lord. It was not because she had taken over for her grandparents five years before, or that she was running late and would have to quickly review her notes for the upcoming sermon. It was not even that her hair still held a faint aroma of sex and marijuana despite washing it. Her anxiousness had every bit of guilt mixed with it.

Pastor Lorraina "Rain" McCall—the holy roller, the counselor, the anointed one, and the head of her church—would have to look one of her members in the eye after service and tell her to 'hang in there' while she finalized a painful divorce. It was the same woman whose husband she had just fornicated with.

"How are you doing, Pastor? Am I interrupting?"

Lorraina jumped with her back facing the office doors. She had been sitting on the edge of her desk and was spraying perfume on her clothes and in her hair to mask the scents of sins.

She must have spoken up the young woman's presence and swallowed hard. Lorraina forced a smile and then shoved her perfume back into her handbag. "Oh, of course not! Hey, Sister Kylie. How are you?"

"I'm okay," the woman said and stepped further in the office. She looked solemn. Her movements were slow, and her voice was just above a whisper as she added, "Capri didn't come home this weekend. I guess it's official; he truly doesn't love me."

Swallowing hard, Lorraina stood from her seat. Her dress had hiked up the longer she sat, and her thick thighs became stuck to the desk. She extended her arms to the woman.

"Aw, baby girl, don't you dare shed a tear," Lorraina instructed. "I told you what's going on. He just needs his time to realize what he has. It's not that he doesn't love you; he has a horrible way of showing it. Give it some time."

"But how much time does he need? He gave me divorce papers, Pastor. I don't think he's trying to work anything out with me. He's probably seeing someone else, and how can I compete with that?"

"Like I said, honey. Give it some time. We have another couple's counseling session coming up soon, and we can talk more about this then," Lorraina grabbed the woman's face and spoke sincerely. Sweat was beginning to form on the top of her lip at Kylie's mention of another woman.

Capri's soon-to-be ex-wife was crying and messing up her beautiful makeup. Lorraina offered Kleenex from the tissue box on her desk and continued, "But for now, get ready to sing your heart out in the choir. Give God the glory! Don't worry about why your husband didn't come home or why he's not here today. You just allow God to move in *your* favor, you hear me?"

"I hear you. I really do."

"Good." Lorraina smiled.

Kylie was in her late twenties and was drop-dead gorgeous with a perfect body. Lorraina could not understand why Capri was taking her for granted, and the guilt plagued her even more.

"Pastor, how do you always know what to say? You're so motherly, sweet, and…Godly! It's like He tells You what to say and do. I pray I can be just like you one day, spiritually," Kylie added on her way out.

Lorraina smiled but did not verbally give her thanks. When the door closed behind her, Lorraina sat down on her leather loveseat and buried her face in her shaky hands. If only Kylie knew just what her beloved pastor had been up to—well into the wee hours of the morning with her husband.

She felt like the bottom of her high heel right now, the lowest of the lows. But this was the life she chose, and she would not change for anything or anyone. Time was winding down, and it was almost time to head out to the pulpit. Lorraina would be tag-teaming with the guest pastor today, and her mind was all over the place. It was truly a wonder how she could effortlessly and effectively deliver the Word of God with so much harboring in her heart.

After taking a deep breath, smoothing out her dress, and then shrugging on her pastoral robe, she marched out of the office to smile, preach, and encourage the people of God.

Chapter One

"Amen. I just want to thank God for the choir and their anointed selections on this morning," the guest pastor, named Stefani, said into the microphone. She had travelled from Texas. She looked over to where Lorraina sat in the pulpit and winked. "I also thank God for that beautiful servant of God. Look at her! Church, y'all are so blessed to be under the leadership of this woman."

Lorraina bowed her head bashfully as her congregants clapped, whistled, and cheered for her. She accepted the compliment and placed a hand over her heart in gratitude. The woman continued to speak and give her regards to the church before she dove into the message. As she spoke, Lorraina's eyes could not help but to drift over the congregation. Her ears tuned out what the speaker was saying and thought back to the sweet nothings that Capri had whispered in her ears last night.

Involuntarily, Lorraina's womanly parts began to yearn for her secret lover. Her temperature began to rise as she thought of his hands in all her sacred places. She thought back to the way he pulled her hair, and the way his hands deeply massaged her skin. A passion mark was just inches below her collarbone even now, and she had to be careful not to move around too much.

There were men and women everywhere. Some were fanning themselves and others were waving their hands in the air at what the visiting pastor was preaching, yet Lorraina could not focus. Her mind was the furthest thing from the King of Kings and the Lord of Lords.

Then, as if a spotlight had been put on her, she jumped as her eyes met a pair of the warmest brown eyes she ever laid eyes on. They belonged to a new member—a man who joined last month and who could not seem to keep his eyes to himself. He seemed to undress her even now as she stared back at him, crossed her leg, and then attempted to look away.

Ten, nine, eight, seven, she counted in her head and then nodded to nothing in particular. *Six, five, four, three, two, one. Is he still staring?* Her thoughts ran wild at the thought that she had an admirer, and a fine one at that.

Her eyes leisurely skimmed back over the crowd and met the stranger's. A smile flirted with her lips. He, too, threw back a smirk. He was still looking hungrily over to where she sat. Garment by garment, he undressed her with his eyes. Lorraina moved around in her seat uncomfortably and licked her lips. This was impossible. His stare was mesmerizing, and already, she was a slave to whatever he had going on with her.

The guy, who looked to be single, had a conservative look but his eyes were far from. Lust dripped from his eyes and sin was literally painted on his expression. He motioned his head over to the exit, and then licked his lips once more. His perfectly sculpted bottom lip became tucked between his teeth. They were straight and as white as the collars around some of the elders' necks. Lorraina could almost smell the richness of his cologne just by staring at him.

Her heart thumped in her chest and the pulse seemed to travel down her body and stop between her legs. No matter how hard she prayed and willed the sensation to go away, she knew that she was in too deep. This mystery man had her intrigued. Her thirst was especially large, and it needed to be quenched. She desired him, although she was in church and now wore her pastoral hat. She longed for him even though she had slept with someone else all weekend. The fire between her legs needed to be put out. He was just the man to do it.

One of Lorraina's lay members stared at her now as she began to sweat uncontrollably and fidget.

"Um, are you okay?" Kylie leaned down low and questioned Lorraina.

"Huh? Oh! Y—yes, I am. I just need a little water please."

"It's right by your chair, Pastor," Kylie added with a look of confusion on her face. "Are you *sure* you're okay?"

Lorraina nodded and then reached for the flimsy water bottle. It crackled loudly under the force of her grabbing it and downing much of its cool contents.

"It's just a hot flash," Lorraina assured her and attempted to smile. "Thank you, honey."

Lorraina swallowed the final bit of water that her throat could handle, and then made the mistake of looking back over at the many faces of the congregation. Her secret admirer was now gone. She could no longer see his broad shoulders, dimpled smile, and neatly trimmed facial hair. As crazy as it sounded, the thought of him leaving unnerved her—it *bothered* her to the core.

Had she scared him away? Had her staring sent him away for good? Was he off to another church, or to gossip about how the pastor had sensually stared him down? She just had to know. With one index finger extended, she disappeared from the pulpit and then scurried to the back of the church.

Lorraina, still wearing her four-inch heels, stammered down the semi-empty hallway. She searched for the missing man like her life depended on it. In a way, she could not believe that she was missing service to follow behind her lustful desires. In the same token, she was certain any woman would have loved to be stared down by such a handsome man. She just had to know his name, if nothing else.

Another five minutes passed before she concluded that he was long gone. He had probably sped off in his vehicle and was now on the phone, calling everyone he knew about their staredown. Lorraina was almost sure that he would not return the next Sunday.

She decided to stop off in her office to freshen her powder foundation and busied herself in the mirror. The guest pastor was still up preaching from what she could hear over the loudspeakers, so she had a few more minutes to get back before the service ended. Lorraina fluffed her hair, puckered her lips, and then turned to the side. She looked good and felt even better.

As she turned to leave out, she ran smack into one of the firmest chests that her breasts had ever been pressed against. Standing at the height of at least 6'5," and looking even more breathtaking up-close was her mystery man. Her eyes dropped to his fingers that were free of any wedding jewelry, and then met his sparkling eyes.

He was amused.

"Were you lookin' for me?"

Lorraina was quiet as she backed away on her heels. Then, she turned and sauntered off into the opposite direction. "Maybe."

"I'm Curtis, but you can call me Curt. I saw you staring out there, so I had to see what the problem was," he said seriously.

Lorraina swallowed the lump in her throat. "No problem at all, and if you noticed me staring, then you were doing the same. Am I right?"

"Yes, you are," he said. His eyes dropped to her body, and he shook his head thoughtfully. "Right and tight. *Goodness*! What did they feed you as a child?"

They exchanged smiles as she continued to walk further into her office closet and then turned on the light.

"Married?"

"Divorced," he answered. "You?"

"It's not for me." She shrugged and began to take off her clothes. Purposely, she left her high heels on while she bent down and stretched out her short but toned legs. Curt looked on in appreciation and leaned against the wall opposite of her.

"Are you coming or what?"

Curt put his hand to his mouth and then bit down on his knuckle. "Should I lock the door...or...?"

"*No*. We can make this quick and be out before offering," Lorraina all but purred.

She looked to the ceiling, prayed for forgiveness for the animinalisic sex she was about to engage in, and then kicked off her heels one by one. It was time to *lay hands* on Curt.

Chapter Two

Curt was as good in bed as Lorraina predicted and they exchanged numbers, so that they could hook up another day. Though she loved the thrill of having sex in her office with the doors unlocked, Lorraina vowed to never do such a thing ever again. After all, her foolish behavior could have been costly in many ways. She sat now, thinking about him, and trying to suppress the smile on her face. It was a few days later and she still wore her same silly, satisfied grin.

"Um, either spill the TEA or snap out of it! Sick of talkin' to you and you're barely saying anything back. What's on your mind? Or should I say, WHO'S on your mind?"

"That's a conversation for another day," Lorraina said simply and licked her lips. She looked up and then mentally shook herself. "What were you saying before?"

"I said, are we doing this or what?"

Lorraina looked to Khloey, her best friend of more than 20 years. Lorraina stood in a tan and white romper that skimmed the curve of her butt, and tan cowboy boots that matched. Her hair was divided into two braids, and a cowboy hat was cocked to the side on her head. She wore only a splash of nude lipstick and a touch of mascara to make her curly eyelashes stand out.

Khloey was similarly dressed for the occasion in a crop top and skintight jeans that hugged her lower half like a pair of denim arms. Instead of cowboy boots, she wore strappy sandals that showed off her pedicured toes. A cowboy hat was also nestled on her head full of dark brown hair. Both women were single and sexily clad with the intentions to have nothing but a fun ladies' night. They were enjoying margaritas at their favorite steakhouse and were both leaned into the booth separating drunken patrons from the mechanical bull. There was a small line for those who wished to mount the machine and Lorraina was at the very front.

Nervously, she watched a platinum blonde-haired white woman with piercing green eyes fall from the bull. Everyone chuckled and cheered around them as the restaurant employee called on the next victim, Lorraina. She swallowed hard. It was now her turn to either embarrass herself or impress all these strangers. Somehow, she felt like the first option would be likely.

"Can we get on together?"

"No." The handsome man shook his head of auburn curls. He favored a young Justin Timberlake. "Just one at a time, sweetheart. Are you ready?"

"I guess," Lorraina sighed, looked to Khloey, and then took his hand. He gently pushed against her butt as she stepped on a stool and then mounted the bull. Quickly, she tightened her legs, and then leaned forward to prepare for the motions. It was uncomfortable but it was something that she always wanted to do, so it was now or never.

"Pull your clothes down, nasty," Khloey yelled. She whipped out her phone with a giggle, ready to record the disaster.

Lorraina tugged at the material that was leaving nothing to the imagination, and just knew she was giving somebody a peep show from behind. *Oh, well*, she thought absent-mindedly. *I've been hittin' my squats lately.*

The employee counted down, and then suddenly Lorraina was hoisted into the air. She moved her hips as the bull moved, leaned as the bull leaned, and kept up as best as she could. The longer she rode, the more the people around her encouraged her.

A few other patrons walked over to admire her skills and a country song played overhead to accompany her gyrating. Ninety percent of the onlookers were men, and they were whistling with appreciation of her thrusting pelvis and rolling hips.

Finally, with a little bit of confidence, Lorraina threw one hand in the air and held onto the hook with the other. The ride slowed down, and much to she and Khloey's surprise, there was no embarrassment. Lorraina breathed a sigh of relief and tilted the brim of her hat playfully while winking at the crowd.

"Way to go! You stayed on all three minutes! Let's give it up for…"

Lorraina looked over to the employee as she carefully hopped down. "Call me Rain."

"Let's give it up for Miss Rain. Not only tiny, but she's beautiful too! You survived the bull, so enjoy your free dessert on us."

She accepted her voucher, and then nudged her friend. "It's your turn."

"Girl, please. You were showing too much booty. Just imagine mine up there. No thanks," Khloey joked, wiggling her bottom half.

Khloey was just as curvy as Lorraina, if not more. The two giggled on their way back to the bar, where they drank a final margarita and ordered dessert before vowing to link back up before the month was out. Lorraina stumbled slightly as she made her way to her truck.

"I'm trying to think back over the last 37 years of my life, and I've honestly *never* seen anything so beautiful."

Lorraina heard the remark, but she did not bother to turn around. Instead, she decided to tease the stranger, "Well, then, I can imagine you want to see me walk some more?"

She walked a moment longer and then glanced over her shoulder.

The guy who was casually walking a couple paces to her right, looked over, and then motioned towards the sky that was painted with purple, magenta, and orange hues. "Oh! I was referring to the sunset. What were *you* talking about?"

Lorraina's cheeks warmed in a blush, and then finally, she looked him in the eye. Her cockiness had caught up to her. Clearly, she was feeling herself, but he was not. "Yes, it is breathtaking."

Suddenly, he was laughing while he joined her side and then cautiously planted his hand on the curve of her back. He was bold, and she could appreciate his confidence.

"Can I walk you to your car?"

"You can, just as long as your hand doesn't go any lower," Lorraina ordered and gave a smile.

He winked. "I would never disrespect that incredible body of yours, Ma."

"*Ma*? Where are you from talkin' like that?"

Lorraina looked him up and down and decided he did not look too crazy. Even in the darkening night, he was striking with his silky, toffee-colored skin, extra white teeth, neatly trimmed facial hair and beard, and chiseled jawline. His well-kept hair was a mixture of curls and short dreadlocks; Lorraina could not decipher. He smelled amazing and wore black diamonds in each of his ears. She was not normally a fan of men having both ears pierced, but he pulled it off in an erotic way.

His tattooed, muscular arms peeked through the wine and gold-colored Kyrie Irving jersey he wore, and she could not remember ever staring into a warmer pair of brown eyes before. Normally, she would call a guy handsome, but this man was absolutely beautiful. He was literally handcrafted by God with precision, patience, and poise. He seemed to know he was good looking as he stared back at Lorraina with his eyebrows raised.

"Are you done?" he teased as he caught her staring.

Lorraina snapped from her daydream. Her gaze had gotten lower and lower on his body. She cursed silently and nodded. "Just thinking."

"To answer your question, I'm originally from New York," he spoke lowly. He shoved his hands into the pockets of his stonewashed jeans. On his feet were wine and gold-colored shoes that looked fresh out of the box. "Yourself?"

"Born and raised in the Sin City," she announced proudly.

"I love it here." He looked around. "I moved here about seven months ago. I was a military brat, so I've lived in eight states. Oh, and for the record? I *was* referring to you. I've never seen a woman so nice-looking before. I just had to mess with your mind a little bit."

"You bruised my ego pretty badly," she said innocently, and pouted her lips. Her light eyes lowered, and her mouth twisted as if she were ready to cry. "And here I was, thinking I'm doing something."

"Trust me." He took her hand and twirled her around. His eyes lingered on her body, and then travelled back up to her eyes. He licked his full lips and continued to hold her hand. "You're definitely doing it and doing it *well*."

"Okay, LL Cool J," she joked.

He chuckled at her comment. "Cute little outfit you have on, too. I saw you workin' the bull in there. That was impressive, so I had to introduce myself."

"And yet, I still don't know your name." The two shook hands. "I'm Lorraina, but I would prefer you call me Rain."

"I'm Jhalil. Jhalil Harrison."

"Nice to meet you," she said sweetly and offered an even sweeter grin.

"Any reason why you prefer to be called Rain?"

Reluctantly, she looked around the empty parking lot, and then back over to him. "I'm a pastor and Lorraina just sounds so formal."

"*Pastor*? Over what?"

"A church, silly." Lorraina stepped backwards towards her truck. "Please don't ask."

He held up his hands. "If pastors were as fine as you back then, I would have been a regular attendee when I was a kid. Instead, I fell off in my middle school days and after my grandmother passed, I stopped going completely."

Lorraina was not sure why he was telling her so much information, but she loved his honesty already. It was obvious why he had followed her out to the parking lot. He was literally devouring her with his eyes.

"What are you doing when you leave here? Bible Study? Prayer service?" Jhalil questioned.

22

He was definitely a jokester; she was learning that more and more. He had now cornered her between her truck door and his body as he leaned with his hand splayed against the tinted passenger window.

"Oh, you're trying to be funny?" Lorraina maneuvered so that she could enter her truck, while she brushed her backside against his body on the way in.

There was just something about this man that was so authentic and refreshing. She was never really one to sleep with anyone on the first night—although the Curt incident had been an exception, but he was tempting her in the worst way. It was like she could not control herself lately; her loins were burning for male attention more than ever.

"Church services are Tuesdays and Sundays, for your information. The rest of the week, I'm doing my own thing," she added.

He motioned towards the restaurant and seemed to relive her mounting the bull. "*Clearly*. I like it though. You're not one of those traditional, long skirt wearin', holier than thou, judgin' pastors."

She smiled and started the engine. It purred like a kitten. "We all fall short from the glory of God, so who am I to condemn? I have no heaven or hell to put anyone in."

"That's deep."

"Just being honest," Lorraina admitted and threw her hat in the back. Then, she fingered one of her long braids. "Where do you stay?"

"Those new townhouses up the street."

"I'll meet you there," Lorraina said simply. She refused to invite him over to her place. She pushed against his chest, closed the door, and watched as he shook his head in amusement.

With anticipation, he nodded to her, and then backed away quickly to get in his own vehicle. The midnight black Lincoln MKX soon joined her on the road, and he flickered his headlights to get her attention. Jhalil switched lanes, taking the lead in front of her, and then rolled his window down to point out the guest parking spaces.

She hopped in the passenger seat of his truck after parking hers, and then he drove them further into his gated community. "This is nice," she commented.

"Thank you," Jhalil said and pulled into the driveway. "You sure you don't want me to go to your place? It'll be late if you decide to leave in the middle of the night."

"Trust me," Lorraina said, "I'm not leaving *anywhere* tonight. Plus, you won't want me to go anywhere when we're done."

"When we're done?" he repeated.

"Isn't that why I'm here?"

There was no shame in her game as she exited his truck and left him speechless. Lorraina knew she was unlike any other woman he had ever been with. Confidently, she walked up to the front door and then looked back at him sassily as if to ask, *what's the hold up?* She sent a text to Khloey about her whereabouts. She was happy that she had shaved this morning, as she followed him into his cozy home.

Chapter Three

"You're not married, are you?" Lorraina leaned in to kiss Jhalil a final time. She was straddling his waist, and they were both still breathing heavily from the sex that had just commenced. The room was stuffy and warm, despite the ceiling fan that was rapidly spinning above their heads.

Jhalil leaned over and grabbed a small remote. With a single button, his central air popped on and cooled their clammy skin immediately. Finally, he looked up to Lorraina, and then laughed. "Isn't it a little too late to be asking questions like that? We've already done the nasty."

Lorraina shook her head. "No, not necessarily. I'm just curious. I don't like ruining happy relationships. It helps to know what I'm up against going into a situationship like this."

"*Situationship?* That's what you ladies call it these days?" He laughed loudly, before she shushed him.

Lorraina, as vocal as she was, had probably disturbed the neighbors while Jhalil sat back and kept a cocky smile on his face.

"Also, consider this," he added. "Was it really a HAPPY relationship, if the man or woman cheats?"

Lorraina cocked her head to the side in thought.

Jhalil shrugged. "I'm just saying."

"So? Are you?" She went back to the question at hand.

"I feel like you've done that before which is why you're asking me. Am I right?" Jhalil reached for something along the nightstand. It was a full, soft box of *Newport* cigarettes. Skillfully, he pulled one out, and then sparked the end of it with his lighter.

Lorraina frowned and pulled the cancer stick from his mouth before he could inhale its toxic contents. "You smoke these? Ew! Who still smokes cigarettes?" she asked and mashed the end of it into an ashtray.

"Obviously me. Why would you do that?" Jhalil gave her an agitated look, and then nudged her off his lap. "These things are expensive."

"Exactly. They're expensive, stink, and are bad for your health. You have pretty teeth; are you trying to ruin 'em?"

Jhalil looked at her incredulously. "Okay, you said you were a pastor, not a health expert. Last time I checked, I was a grown man who could make his *own* decisions in his *own* house."

"You're absolutely right, but you are in the company of someone who's asthmatic. Can you please refrain from that crap while I'm here?"

He blew out hot air, and then gave in. He tucked his bottom lip between his teeth and then nodded. "Alright, but only 'cause I like you."

"You like *me*, or do you like what I can do to and for your body? We barely know each other," Lorraina said and climbed back onto his lap.

"Nah, I like *you*. I think I want to marry you after what just took place," he confessed, only half serious.

They shared knowing smiles and then leaned into one another. Jhalil's hand came up to cup the back of her head, as he kissed her sloppily. His other hand smoothed over her stomach.

Her body was nothing short of amazing to him. She looked nothing like what he normally slept with or hung out with. He was normally into the tiny, petite women, but Lorraina was far from a size four, or even a size eight. If he had to guess, he'd say Lorraina was a healthy size 12. Her body was toned to perfection, complete with curves and the right amount of jiggle.

She brought his hand up to her face where she nestled her cheek against it.

"You tryin' to start something else?" he asked.

His hands fell to her knees as he held her in place. Her ample thighs were spread, and he noticed the inked artwork along her legs. There was just something about a female with tattoos that attracted him. So many people thought it was classless, but Jhalil found it endearing.

"I've already started something, from the moment you saw me," she said seductively.

Jhalil gently rolled Lorraina onto her back and wedged his body between her legs. His fingers outlined her nose, cheekbones, and lips. Wisps of hair had escaped her French braids and were curling against her forehead because of the moisture.

"You are breathtaking," he whispered huskily. His hand came up and closed around her neck while he made a meal out of the sensitive skin at her earlobe. "Like for real. You're a masterpiece—my own little Mona Lisa."

Lorraina giggled in flirtation, and he could feel her body crying out for him again. But he sensed that something was on her mind as she pulled back to look at him. "But seriously, you're not married, are you?"

Jhalil grew quiet and his kisses halted. He stared into her eyes and removed his hand from around her neck. He figured it was best to be truthful. "I'm not married, but I am seeing someone."

He could literally feel the disappointment flow from Lorraina, while they stared each other down. He felt bad suddenly, since he had gone into this "situationship" as a free agent. But she couldn't be totally mad at him. It wasn't like they were trying to dive into a relationship.

"Oh," she said simply.

"Hey, don't do that," Jhalil demanded. "This was nice. I want to do it again. We're not engaged or married. She and I are just friends who sleep together and have a longstanding history with each other. I care for her but there's no love between us. No need to catch an attitude," he explained.

"I'm not catching an attitude. I just wished I had asked before we did this, you know?"

Lorraina attempted to move from his embrace, but he held her down. Her hands were captive in his grasp, and his strength weighed her down deliciously. Jhalil buried his head in the crook of her neck and began to make passion marks along her flushed collarbone and down to the tops of her breasts. She moaned into the atmosphere and squirmed under his touch.

"Would tellin' you that I was seeing someone upfront have changed anything?"

She thought his words over, even though he made it hard to concentrate. Jhalil moved further down her body, and he eventually disappeared underneath the mangled, black sheets.

"Hmm? I asked you a question," Jhalil commanded lowly. His vocal cords rumbled against the bottom of her stomach.

"No."

"Would you still have come home with me?"
He gently bit the sensitive skin of her inner thighs.
"Yes," she admitted in a whisper-moan.
"Alright. I thought so."

***

Time with Jhalil was well spent. What was thought to be one night of fun and passion turned into an entire week of calling in and delaying work-related duties for both Jhalil and Lorraina. She learned a lot about him, from his pet peeves, to when he had his first kiss, to his favorite sports teams, and even his most embarrassing childhood memory as a 10-year-old.

Jhalil had many layers and sides to him that she could appreciate. He was a corporate businessman who had a whole lot of swag and impact in the community. He also volunteered each summer to coach a local peewee football team and had no children. In addition to all that good stuff, he was an incredible cook, or so he proclaimed. She had yet to sample his culinary creations.

The thing that struck her the most was, like Lorraina, he was deeply rooted in his faith. While their actions were less than holy, he still understood the Bible from front to back and valued his relationship with God. She respected that.

Other than this mystery woman that he mentioned he was *casually* dating, Jhalil was perfect. His company was calming, and their conversations were natural. It was like they had known each other for years.

She would be remiss not to share her own life with him after he poured his heart out to her, so she revealed a few things to him too from her family dynamics to her desire to one day have a big family, and even to how much pressure she felt week after week as a shepherd of the Christian church. However, as the woman and more vulnerable of the two, she kept her heart and mind guarded. When the time was right, and if they even made it past the week of seeing each other, she planned to give him more and more of herself as time went on.

After a few days of exploring each other's bodies, streaming movies, and enjoying takeout, Jhalil drove Lorraina out to the strip. They shopped at The Forum Shops at Caesar's Palace, ate at the Eiffel Tower restaurant, and then caught a magic show at the MGM Grand. Lorraina literally had so much fun and enjoyment that she lied to her assistant pastor about being sick, so she would not have to preach for Bible Study. Her lying was wrong, but Jhalil's company felt so right.

It was now Saturday evening, and they sat across from each other in her condo. She had given him her body, and now he had access to her home as she told him where her spare key was early in the day. While she ran to complete a few errands, Jhalil volunteered to cook her dinner. When she returned, a number of delicious aromas greeted her nostrils and made her tummy do a backflip. She was shocked to say the least.

"I guess you *can* cook. It smells so good," she told him and hugged his waist. Her palms flattened against his rock-hard abdomen.

Jhalil was sporting comfortable loungewear; he loved joggers and wore a grey pair with its matching hooded sweatshirt. "You hungry?" he asked.

"I am. What is this? You seriously cooked all *that?*" Lorraina peeked around his body to investigate each of the pots and pans staring back at her.

He tucked Lorraina under his arm as he pointed and explained each of his creations. "Last but not least, this is pan-seared trout with Italian-style salsa. I hope you like everything."

"I'm sure I will."

They sipped on a red wine as they ate, and conversation was light and playful. A comedy movie played in the background.

"So, I need your opinion on something."

"Sure." Lorraina smiled and cleaned the table off.

Jhalil fingered his wineglass and cleared his throat. "I, um, I broke up with my lady friend."

Silence.

"Are you goin' to say something?" Jhalil laughed lightly and asked.

"What am I supposed to say?" Lorraina shrugged and settled back in her seat. "'*Congrats*'? Why did you do it?"

He studied her for a long moment. "Honestly? We weren't making much progress and lately, you and I have been kickin' it pretty hard. I just wanted to see where this takes us, you know? I'm not going to lie. You're making me do some crazy things, shorty."

"Oh, am I?" she flirted. "Crazy things like what? It's only been a week." She giggled.

Her ego was through the roof at his confessions, and she felt warm and tingly inside. But a part of her felt nervous that he'd broken things off with his friend. Why was he putting so much trust in their sexual relationship?

Jhalil pulled his bottom lip between his teeth with one of the cutest expressions she had ever seen, and then tugged on her wrists. She settled between his legs, and he palmed her backside while he continued to speak.

"I've broken up with a female, taken off an entire workweek for you at the busiest time of my firm; I even spent a third of my paycheck to ensure you smiled during our time together. Not to mention, I *rarely* cook for anyone, much less a woman I barely know," Jhalil added. "What are you doing to me?"

Lorraina was speechless. She giggled sweetly, and then held her hand over her heart. "Stop it."

"No, seriously, you've blown my mind. So, I guess I just have to know since I'm going all in."

"What's that?"

"Are there any people that I should know about? Are you seeing anyone? What am *I* up against?"

Quickly, she weighed the options in her mind. She thought about Capri and their unorthodox history. At some point, she planned to break things off with him, so she figured his name didn't even need to come up in the conversation.

"No, I'm as single as that cigarette sitting in the ashtray," she said good-naturedly, and they shared a laughed.

"I was never into titles, but we'll see where this takes us. Just please be honest with me. That's all I ask," Jhalil added. "As long as *we* have an understanding, that's all that matters. You got me?"

"I got you, sexy," she promised and climbed on top of his lap.

"Alright, now give me some of those sweet lips," he murmured.

As much as she wanted him to stay over, tomorrow was Sunday, and she would have to preach. Lorraina said her goodbyes, briefly went over her notes for the sermon, and then slept peacefully with the lingering scent of Jhalil in her pillows, sheets, and against her skin.

Chapter Four

Lorraina's sermon, the next day, went well. Twelve people surrendered their lives to God, and three new families joined her church. She noticed that a few members were not in attendance, but she figured it was because of the rainstorm that now drenched the city. It was like an ocean had been dispensed over the city of Las Vegas. There was a flash flood warning and the news stations warned of oil buildups on the roads. Church normally lasted an hour and a half, but Lorraina had let out after just forty minutes to protect her congregants. She rushed home with Jhalil's voice blaring through her car's Bluetooth system.

Despite the weather, he wanted to see her as if he had not spent the last few days with her. He told her how much he missed her and within an hour, was standing before her with bags of takeout food, a couple of romance and comedy movies, and lust-filled eyes. He wanted to do more than just relax with a good movie and delicious Chinese food. She was game for whatever he had planned.

"So, what is this? I know we've discussed this before, but what are we doing exactly?" Jhalil questioned.

"We're chilling. What do you mean?"

"You know exactly what I mean," he said and bit into the shrimp and vegetable eggroll. "Are we just going to be friends and have this amazing sex? Or are we going to be exclusive and put a title with this? I just want to know before I say something I regret."

"Say something like what?"

"I just can't explain the...the feelings I have for you. You've got my head all in the clouds, and

I'm not just saying this to trick or confuse you. I genuinely have love for you, Lorraina, and I want to see where things go. Am I alone in this?"

She was shocked as she began to choke on the bean sprouts in her fried rice.

"You okay?"

He handed her the can of soda that he was sipping on. The beverage did not agree with her stomach either and she was forced to stand up and hold her stomach. As she rushed to the bathroom, she planted both hands down on the sink and attempted to rid her throat of the rice that seemed to stick to her tonsils.

"Oh, my goodness!"

Jhalil, who had rushed in behind her, patted her back a few times while she composed herself. Her nose started to run, and her eyes became watery. She felt like the snotty-nosed kid, Roscoe, from The Martin Lawrence show.

"So?"

"So, what?" She looked at him through the mirror and cleared her throat.

"Am I in this alone?"

Lorraina rubbed her chest and coughed a few more times.

"I guess that's a no," he said, and she could hear the attitude in his tone.

"Can I finish choking?" she snapped at him. "I...I can't even breathe and you're wanting me to answer questions?"

"You're talking now."

"Jhalil, don't do this," Lorraina said and coughed. "Please don't act like that."

"How am I acting? It's just crazy that I've been vulnerable and honest, but you're avoiding your feelings for me, and I have a problem with that."

Lorraina could not believe Jhalil's behavior. She was literally a step away from performing the Heimlich maneuver on herself, yet he wanted to accuse her of avoiding a serious discussion. Not only that, but he was acting like they had been dating for months and months. It had literally only been a week since she met him. As she wiped her eyes and dabbed her nostrils with Kleenex, she looked over to him in disbelief.

"I'm okay, if you cared to know."

"Look, I'm not trying to be difficult, and obviously I'm concerned about your breathing, but…"

Lorraina stood to her full height and walked back out to the living room. She plopped down on the couch and tucked her legs under her buttocks. She was no longer hungry, thirsty, or in the mood to spend this gloomy evening with him.

"Let yourself out and don't slam my door."

"Are you serious right now?" he questioned.

"No, are YOU serious right now? You want to put me on a guilt trip while I'm choking on FOOD, and then get angry when I can't answer? You sound ridiculous. If this is how you react over something so little, then we can't be together."

"Well, according to you, we're not together at all. We're just friends with benefits. We're too old for the games, Lorraina. This isn't high school. Just let me know how you're feeling."

"Aren't you the same one that said you don't do titles? Why is this such a big deal? Why can't we just take this one day at a time and figure it out down the line?"

"Because I'm in love with you!" he yelled and slammed his hand down on the back of the couch. "I've FALLEN in love with you, I'm IN love with you, and I want to BE with you! Haven't my actions proven that? Why can't you understand that?"

Lorraina swallowed the lump in her throat and kept her eyes low. She knew he was interested in her, but she never imagined it was love—especially so soon. This was almost unheard of.

He looked so sincere as he went on and on about how much she had impacted his life in a short time, and all she could think about was the rain that was thumping against her rooftop.

"Am I in this alone? Where's your head at?" he asked for the tenth time.

She could not say she had an answer for him. She enjoyed his company and she had missed him in the short time they were away, but she still was not sure about how she felt. She was used to getting hurt, and he was probably no exception. Being so fine and put together, he was probably a heartbreaker. Although he talked a good game, she was not going to take any chances on love until she was good and ready.

"You're not in this alone," she assured him. "We're in a really good place. But I don't want to put a title on anything just yet."

Jhalil breathed heavily and looked like he wanted to cry. He was frustrated and his sexiness soared. The way his chiseled jawline tightened was attractive, and the sound of his raspy voice struck a nerve in her womanly parts. She knew just the thing to wipe the frown off his face.

"Come here."

"I'm not trying to do all that. I want to talk to you and figure this thing out."

"So, let's figure it out," she spoke breathily. She wanted to tease him into submission. She was uncomfortable with where this conversation was going and just wanted to be done with it. "What do you love about me? Is it my thighs?"

"Rain, seriously? Why are you——?" he began to ask, but she cut him off.

"Why am I turning you on so much? Hmm?" Lorraina stood up and untied the robe until it fell around her frame. Beneath the satin material was a pair of boyshorts and a camisole that rode up on her midriff. "Why am I so sexy to you?"

It was Jhalil's turn to swallow hard. The sound was so loud that it echoed throughout the room. He looked her up and down and seemed to think things over in his head. Then suddenly, he growled and cornered her against the wall.

She had him.

***

The week had flown by, and her couple's counseling sessions rolled around with the Jordans. She sat cross-legged with a notepad in her hands, while Capri and Kylie sat on the opposite ends of her loveseat.

Lorraina's corner office was cool from the oscillating fan. Purposely, she wore layers to deter Capri's eyes from drifting while they talked for the next hour and a half. A thin turtleneck fully covered her C-cup breasts; its gray material was itchy and flimsy. On her legs were black slacks, and her low pumps gave her a conservative look.

The McCall Worship Center was closed so that she could speak with this young couple about their marital issues. She had popped a muscle relaxer to prepare for this session. It was unlike any other. After all, she was counseling the same man that she was sexing, along with his wife, who was one of her closest associates. It was truly uncomfortable.

Whenever they discussed intimacy, she and Capri's eyes would meet. Kylie brought up the possibility of another woman and expressed how crushed she would be if that were the case. As they wrapped up their session, Kylie grew inquisitive.

"Pastor, can I ask you something?"

"Of course, honey." She placed her notepad beside her and removed her glasses. "Ask me anything."

"Were you ever married?"

"No." Lorraina shook her head. "I've been in relationships, but nothing ever grew serious. It was like a defense mechanism. I just sort of gave up on love."

"Why is that?" Kylie questioned. "Why did you give up on love?"

Lorraina swallowed the lump in her throat. She had been dreading answering such a question because she knew exactly where it would lead her. Kylie looked on with her almond-shaped eyes, and Capri fidgeted uneasily. "Well, I've been cheated on quite a few times, and I figured, it was better to guard my heart than to give it away."

Kylie turned to Capri, widening her eyes. "See? You want me to end up like that? No offense, Pastor, but baby, the way you hurt me, I'm at this point. Can you honestly say you want me to have that kind of mindset? Better yet, if you had a daughter, would you want her to hurt the way that I hurt? No! You'd be ready to kill someone for cheating on your daughter, don't lie!"

"Well, maybe if you knew how to treat a man, it wouldn't be so easy for me to step out! All you do is nag and complain! A man needs to be respected and treated like a king!"

"And a woman doesn't need to be spoiled? There you go with the double standards again."

Lorraina held up her hand and attempted to bring peace to the situation. "Calm down, you two, and please don't talk over each other."

Capri spoke up this time and eyed Lorraina with a knowing look. "Pastor, can I ask you something this time?"

He had a look in his eyes that made her skeptical to hear about his next words. "Um, sure."

"How would you please your man to keep him? I mean, surely, you may not have been married before, but you've *been* with a man before. You weren't always saved." He winked.

Shocked, Lorraina started to choke on nothing. She looked over to the water bottle that seemed so far from her reach. She rushed to go grab the lukewarm liquid, so that it could moisten her parched throat. "That's uh, I believe that is an inappropriate question."

"How so?" he inquired and one of his eyebrows was higher than the other in thought. "We've told you our deepest secrets. Surely, you can teach her a thing or two about what to do and what *not* to do in the bedroom. After five years, she still hasn't learned ANYTHING!"

Kylie burst into tears and ran out of the office, while Capri shook his head and watched her in dispassion. He was so disconnected from her and lacked any type of empathy. Lorraina waited for the door to close before slamming her hand down on her thigh. "Are you serious right now? Why are you humiliating her?"

"She's always playing the victim, and I'm sick of it!" Capri exclaimed.

He stood up and snatched Kylie's purse along the way. "I'm not staying with her. I don't care about your outlook on divorce. I don't want to be with that woman. If she's not you, I don't want any part of it."

"SHHH!"

"Naw, that's the problem. I'm tired of having to keep my mouth closed. Why is it always about the woman and what she wants? Why can't a man express his feelings without him being viewed as aggressive or insensitive? That woman hasn't made love to me in over a year. We're just going through the motions, and I hate it now. I can't do this anymore," Capri whispered his final words. "Why can't I be with you? You KNOW how I feel about you, Rain."

Lorraina looked towards the door and pleaded with her eyes. "Do not do this. Please don't do that. You know exactly why we can't be together."

"No, I actually don't. I know why *you* say we can't be together. We must live by a standard that you're not even following. You pull the religion card when it's most convenient for you. Yet you're having sex, you're cursing and drinking, and you're doing God only knows what else."

"That's how you feel, huh? You've wanted to say that for the longest I'm guessing? What else, Capri? You want to air out our dirty laundry too when she comes back?"

"Whatever, Rain." Capri waved his hand in dismissal and reached for the doorknob.

Kylie opened the door at the same time, and still looked pained from her husband's words and antics. "I'm sorry for leaving out, but this is what I'm talking about. Everything is always about him. If he's not being pleased, or not getting his way, he likes to play the blame game. I just don't know what else to do."

"Sit down. Both of you." Lorraina pointed to the loveseat. She waited until they were both seated before continuing, "I know it's easier said than done, but you two MUST learn how to work through your differences and see where the other is coming from. Capri, she's feeling ignored and unappreciated. Kylie, he's feeling unwanted and unsatisfied."

Lorraina could not believe she was saying her next words.

"This is coming from someone who has heard countless stories. Sex is not everything in a marriage, Capri. Yes, it's important but it's not everything. It's about enjoying your partner, and loving them, flaws and all. In the same token, Kylie, sometimes as women we get so caught up in how we desire to be treated that we force unrealistic expectations on our spouses. This can be worked through with time, but the question is, are you two willing to work at it?"

Kylie, who was still shedding a few tears of embarrassment, nodded 'yes.' Capri shook his head 'no.'

"Why not?"

"Because I'm in love with someone else!" Capri stood up and screamed. "HAPPY now? Man, I'm out!"

Lorraina's jaw hit the floor, and Kylie's cries grew louder. Just before leaving the office, Capri turned and challenged Lorraina. "You seem to have so much advice and yet, you're sleeping around with how many people? You've been single for how long? Thank you for your advice, Pastor, but I'm signing those papers."

Lorraina was speechless as she watched him walk out. She gritted her teeth in anger and felt her skin grow hot with irritation. As she consoled Kylie, she vowed never to sleep with Capri ever again. He had purposely waited for their counseling session to profess his love to her, and he had done it in such a way that, if Kylie weren't so naïve and emotional, she could have instantly caught onto what he was implying.

She decided to give him a piece of her mind just as soon as she left the church. He answered on the first ring.

"Are you kiddin' me? What was that about?"

"You know what? You're lucky I didn't expose you. How dare you keep pressing the issue of working things out? I told you already, I want out of that marriage. I want YOU."

"And I've told you already that you cannot have me, Capri. What would people think or say? That wouldn't be a good look, and you know it. I've smiled in that girl's face time and time again. How would that make me look?"

"We're already together, just without the title. I'm not trying to see you every blue moon. I want to wake up to you, kiss you every morning, and lay next to you every night," Capri whined. "Who cares what people think anyway? You, yourself, have preached about the dangers of judging others. They can kick rocks for all I care. I just want *you*."

"I'll talk to you another day," Lorraine said above a whisper.

There was no point in coaxing him to change his way of thinking. She regretted ever laying down with him and ever sharing pillow talk with him. He was turning this sexual relationship into something deeper than what it was.

She needed to vent to someone. Khloey had no idea that she sleeping with a married man, so that was out of the question. She chose to dial the infamous ten numbers that soon connected her to a sensual baritone.

"Can you please make me feel better?" she begged.

"What's wrong?"

"Just…make me feel better," she repeated.

As Jhalil took her body to ecstasy, less than an hour later, her mind drifted back to her sweet yesteryears when there were no strings attached, and no hearts were being broken. There was no trust being questioned, there were no false promises, no sex partners, and there was nothing but purity and innocence surrounding her.

She longed for those days again.

Chapter Five

September 1999

Lorraina sang along to Destiny's Child's "Bug A Boo" while two of her good friends from high school harmonized with her.

Dressed to kill in matching thigh-length leather skirts, crop tops that bared their newly pierced navels, and with pounds of makeup caked on their young features, it was clear that they were the freshest women in the college party.

Excitement flowed through their veins for what was about to go down, while their eyes raced around the room to see the who's who of the University of Nevada-Las Vegas. Lorraina watched as a group of uppity but gorgeous sorority girls gathered to step, while a team of football players strolled through the room looking for willing females to take back to their dorm rooms.

Although it was in-state, she planned to attend the university next year, and was working hard towards securing scholarships and building trust in her family so that she could live on campus. Lorraina could practically taste her freedom, and it was making her wish she were just a year or two older.

"He is fine!" One of the girls pointed out, and all three heads turned in sync. They focused on the upperclassman who looked like he was close to seven feet tall. Tucked under an arm was a basketball, and his hands were large as he waved to women here and here. They looked like they could palm more than just the sports equipment.

Licking her lips and then swallowing hard, Lorraina watched his every move. He greeted everyone, smiled charismatically, and then looked to her. Instead of ignoring her like the remainder of the men in the party, he seemed to like what he was focusing on. Without time to freshen her breath with gum or mints, Lorraina looked to her friends, and then back at the approaching athlete.

She was just shy of five feet and stared at him, from his size 15 shoes to his slightly baggy jeans, to his basketball jersey, and then to his impressive half-smile. He must have been a brace face once upon a time because his teeth were too perfect.

"You go to UNLV?"

Lorraina swallowed hard and thought her options over. He could have been campus security for all she knew, or he could have seriously been interested in her. She spoke carefully and softly, "No."

"Thought so. I've never seen you around campus before," the nameless guy nodded to Lorraina's giggling friends. "What's up, ladies? Y'all want to chill over there with me and some of the fellas?"

There was no hesitation or objection from any of the girls. Not even a half-hour later, Lorraina sat on the basketball player's lap. His name was TJ, and apparently, he was a beast on the courts. Her friends, Khloey and Shawanna, were nestled under the men of their choices. The night could not have gone any better. Their fake IDs had not been questioned, the basketball players weren't disrespectful and had been super cool to hang with, and Lorraina's phone had not rang once with her grandmother on the other end.

Her months of planning had truly paid off. Plus, she planned to give her number to the good-looking brotha playing in her hair. But within milliseconds, her confidence, energy, and world was interrupted.

"Lorraina Belle McCall, get your behind off of that young man right this second!"

The 17-year old's ears perked up, hearing the voice of her grandmother, who was the senior pastor and co-founder of The McCall Worship Center. It was the same church that Lorraina should have been attending for tonight's service, but instead, she had lied to her grandmother and said she was sick.

Once she'd gotten the clearance to stay in from service, Lorraina had packed an overnight bag, made up her bed to resemble a sleeping body, and then had scurried off with her friends to the college party that everyone had raved about. Friday youth services normally lasted well into the wee hours of the morning, and yet, staring back at Lorraina was her grandmother. Clearly, she had spoken too soon, and her planning was crumbling before her very eyes.

Upperclassmen near and far 'oohed' as they assumed she was in trouble, and then made jokes about her while she scrambled to find where the voice was coming from. There were just a few things that could get Hattie Mae McCall upset. Talking back of any kind, leaving a chore undone, and hanging around with boys were all at the top of the list. Fear set in Lorraina's young heart, as she knew she had been caught doing the latter.

Without a care in the world, the rambunctious teenager had taken off her high heels, and had thrown both legs over TJ's. The already short skirt now favored panties, as it hiked up against Lorraina's widening thighs. TJ, who had been kissing along her earlobe, looked up at her grandmother and frowned. His eyebrows were bunched together as he nodded to Hattie.

"Can we help you?"

Lorraina eased from TJ's hold, much to his dismay and confusion. She tugged helplessly at the crop top to cover her stomach, but it was no point. Her skin was exposed, and her grandmother had seen it all, including the bellybutton piercing. Perhaps that was the reason Grandma Hattie's yell was laced with frustration and anger. It could have also had something to do with Lorraina's virgin body that was being violated by a much older man.

"What did I say? Gather your clothes and come on, 'fore I pull off this big ol' belt and teach you some respect for yourself! Little Lorraina, you've got FIVE seconds!"

Whenever her grandmother called her "Little Lorraina," it meant that things were serious. Lorraina snatched up her scattered garments, waved a sad goodbye to her friends, and then held her head down. She was sure to be the joke of the party, and the only partygoer whose guardian had burst in and made a scene.

On the way past her grandmother, Lorraina felt the worst pain on this side of heaven. It was the pop of her grandmother's hand to her backside, and she was certain that, hours later, there would be an imprint or bruise of some sort.

Once they got out of the Student Union, her grandmother continued to yell. She was still dressed conservatively in a long, blue jean skirt and white, orthopedic shoes. "Chile, what have I told you about playing games with me? Something told me to check on you at home, and all that was in your bed were pillows. On top of that, you LIED to me. How could you? I thought you could be trusted!"

All Lorraina's life, she had been trained, sheltered, and taught to live above a higher standard than her peers, but she could not see what the big deal was. This time was no exception as she prayed that her cell phone would not be taken away from her. Granted, she had lied and feigned sickness, but she was certain her grandmother would have flat out told her 'no' had she told the truth.

"I ought to spank you in front of all them people! Look at your clothes! You were sitting on a grown man's lap! You had no business at this party," her grandmother continued, and popped her bottom a final time. "Look at me."

Lorraina whipped around with tears brimming her somber eyes. Like the mother that she had never met, Lorraina's eyes were slanted exotically at the corners, and her button nose began to run. Her slightly moist curls were frizzy and now sticking up in every direction, and her butt stung as if she had been burned with fire.

"Baby, I don't mean to make you cry, but you have to realize you are one of the church's praise dancers, and you will someday be great in life."

Lorraina's cheek was caressed as her caregiver embraced her.

When she was just three months old, Lorraina's mother had met some drug-dealing thug one weekend and had run off with him. Lorraina had never known her father, and on top of that, she was an only child. Her grandmother was the only parent and family member that Lorraina knew, and although stern, she had a heart of gold. Her hugs were especially warm, and her kisses were sweet and plentiful. She also cooked the best food that Lorraina's palate had ever been blessed with.

"But Grandma, why are you so hard on me? I am almost in college. No one else my age is treated like this. All year, I keep up my grades, do my chores, and I never get to do ANYTHING. I just don't get it."

"I know you're almost in college, baby, but you're not like the other kids. You will preach to nations, and impact other women with your words and lifestyle. You can't be runnin' around and chasin' these little boys who only want ONE thing anyway. What kind of message would that send to people? God didn't create you to be no hussy," Hattie Mae explained gently.

"Hussy? I was just having a little fun. I wasn't going to sleep with anybody." Lorraina's face was screwed up in defense.

"I sure hope you weren't, but Lawd knows, what I saw tonight made me question it all. Just promise me one thing, and one thing only."

Lorraina wiped the mucus from her nostrils and then blinked back any tears that threatened to spill over onto her beautifully sculpted cheekbones. "Yes, ma'am?"

"You stay away from those boys. Don't start lying to me either, and you stay away from those fast-tailed friends of

*yours. It just doesn't look good to people who don't know you
for the queen you are. You have to be ladylike, you hear me?"*
*She tugged on Lorraina's skirt. "And remember, whenever you
have a dress or skirt on, I don't EVER want to see your leg in
the air or thrown on top of a man's. Your body belongs to
God, until He sends your husband. Do I make myself clear?"*

"Yes, ma'am," Lorraina answered softly.

*"That's all I ask." Hattie Mae led her only
grandchild to the station wagon parked in front of the
university. They held hands and looked into each other's eyes
lovingly. Forgiveness had been granted that night.*

*"I love you, Lorraina. I promise, if you stay faithful
and keep your eyes on God, you'll be a very happy woman."*

"Huh?"

"Lorraina?"

A warm, soapy cloth landed on her lap as
she yelled out and came back to reality. Jhalil stood
above Lorraina shrugging his undershirt on and
chuckling.

"Huh?" she questioned again with
confusion.

"Are you okay?"

Lorraina blinked away the forming tears and
hid her expression from him. Her head dipped
forward, and her hair covered her face from his
view, just as she wanted it to. It was not his business
to know why she was so upset, nor did she have the
strength to explain how badly she was feeling.
"Yeah. Just thinkin'."

Her heart dropped as she realized that she
had disappointed her grandmother in every way.
Everything that she had promised her grandmother
on her deathbed had been a lie. She had not stayed
a virgin until marriage; she had not kept her
"temple" free of sin, and oftentimes, slept away her
pain of losing the only constant thing in her life.

Lorraina had broken up happy homes and was involved with married and committed men. Plus, she was no longer taking her preaching responsibilities as seriously as she should have.

She was a mess.

She missed her grandmother dearly, and it was times like these, where she wanted to drop by or simply call to hear her grandmother's hearty laughter and motherly advice.

"I'm so sorry," Lorraina whispered.

She planned to go to her grandmother's gravesite this weekend. She had a lot to confess and think about.

Jhalil watched as she wiped her teary eyes, and quietly wiped herself clean from their sexual intercourse. "Shorty, what are you apologizin' for? What's wrong?"

"Nothing's wrong." Lorraina smiled as she draped the washcloth on the headboard, and then began to pull on her slacks. "You were perfect."

Jhalil did not look convinced, but he stepped forward. He was in his boxer-briefs and a ribbed tank top. Warmly, he pulled her into his strong arms and kissed her as though they were a couple in love.

The kiss was simple but promising, and as he pulled away, Jhalil whispered, "I feel it, too."

"You feel what?"

"Sometimes I think God's not done with me yet. Sometimes I think I've let Him down, and I just go off on tangents and lose myself. That same guilt you're feeling right now...I feel it too," he said shakily. "All I'm asking, ma, is that you pray for me as I pray for you."

"Of course." She rubbed the sides of his jawline, studying him. "Is everything okay?"

He took her hands from his face, squeezing them gently.

"And in the meantime," he paused, looking off into space for a moment, "let's just slow down. Let's...let's take a break, and figure out where we are because it's obvious, we aren't seeing things eye to eye anymore."

Lorraina's eyes narrowed as he sidestepped her. She watched his back as he moved purposely around the room. "Okay...so where does that leave us? Are you calling it quits?"

"I'm not calling it quits—not that we have established anything to even give it a name. I'm just saying, let's just cool it for a little bit while you figure things out for yourself. You've made it clear you don't feel how I feel for you, and I'm not even sure you know what *you* want. So...let's just...cool it down." He shrugged as though it were so simple.

"Okay..."

Jhalil pulled on a casual T-shirt. When his head reappeared through the shirt's opening, his eyes found hers immediately. "We can continue to call each other and check in on each other, but let's remove the sex and see what we have."

Lorraina wasn't sure what to say or what to do. She didn't understand his approach, since it was understood on night one that their "relationship" was sex-based and lust-driven. Who said anything about falling in love or pursuing anything? Why was emotionless sex so hard for the men in her life?

She scratched a small itch on her shoulder, and then reluctantly followed his lead with getting dressed. She had no more energy to try to sort everything out when the arrangements made total sense to her. She would give him space, as he asked, and see where life took them. It was all she could do.

Chapter Six

Jhalil's request stayed with Lorraina as they succeeded in going a few weeks without seeing one another. Though they checked in by text and email, and talked periodically on the phone, sex was now a distant memory. She drowned herself in her ministerial work and was blessed with a speaking engagement for an upcoming women's conference later in the year. Additionally, God blessed her with the opportunity to write a 30-day devotional for single women, and she was on top of her game.

For once in her adult life, she was not confused and wondering what her next moves were. Lorraina had successfully weaned Capri away, and did not plan to ever go back to him. But when he sent her a text message asking to gain closure and nothing more, she accepted. After their few years of fooling around, it was the least that he deserved, and she was willing to answer his questions.

They decided to meet at the grocery store. It was Lorraina's idea since she needed to purchase a few items anyway, and she refused to allow him to come back to her place. She grabbed a cart and waited near the produce section. He pulled up outside not long after.

"Hey," she said dryly.

Capri reached in for a hug, to which Lorraina granted. It was brief, cold, and would be her last.

"How are you, beautiful?"

"Cut it out. Don't start with the compliments or the sweet talk," she threatened. "I just want to get to the bottom of this, buy my groceries, and be done with all of this."

"Why are you acting like that? You act like I cheated on you, and I owe you an apology. We both were in the wrong, so why are you treatin' me like this?" Capri questioned as he followed behind her.

Lorraina leaned slightly into the cart and pushed it leisurely. Her eyes and focus were ahead of her, but her words were directed towards him.

"I'm acting like this because you forgot what we agreed upon when we started this affair. You seem to have forgotten that agreement and the fact that it doesn't matter how close we've gotten over the years, I do not want a relationship with you or anyone. You *know* that, Capri," she explained and reached for a pack of ground turkey. As she checked the freshness of it, he smacked his lips beside her.

"You can't control who you fall in love with, and that's exactly what happened for me, baby. Of course, I remember our agreement, but you can't say you don't feel anything for me."

Lorraina looked over at him and shook her head. "I *can* say that. I don't feel anything other than attraction towards you. Even if I was feeling some type of way towards you, what about your little episode during our counseling session? You practically ran everything down to Kylie, and that wasn't cool. For that reason, I have to separate myself from you."

"That's foul, Lorraina. So that's *really* the reason you want to break this off? I don't believe that!" Capri exclaimed and his voice grew louder with each word.

"First of all, lower your voice. And two, you're absolutely right. That's not the only reason I'm breakin' up with you and haven't been returning your calls."

Lorraina walked over to the fruits and vegetables and gathered a couple in her arms. She avoided his eyes as she placed the food in plastic bags. "I'm in love with someone else."

It was the first time that she acknowledged her feelings for Jhalil, and it honestly felt good. She wouldn't dare smile though, knowing that her words had further upset Capri.

"Who is he?"

"You don't know him, and I'm not giving you any details either. Just know that what we had was special while it lasted. I wouldn't trade it for anything else in the world, but it's time to finally part ways, Capri," Lorraina paused and chose her next words carefully. "I hope you understand and can move forward without me."

That seemed to be all Capri needed to hear to cause the tears to well up in his disappointed eyes.

"Nah. I'm not accepting that at all. Are you kiddin' me right now?"

Lorraina watched as he did the last thing she expected him to do. With one clean swipe, he brought his arm up and slapped the items from her grasp. Grapes, apples, and bell peppers flew to the ground with soft thuds, and all the attention was turned to them instantly.

Along with the produce, her phone fell on the ground and Capri wasted no time in snatching it before she could pick it up. He meddled with her lock screen, placed it to her face, and then smirked as her phone became unlocked. He scrolled through it for a few quick moments, going through pictures and contacts, and then finally found text messages between her and Jhalil.

Capri's voice was a mixture of pain and humiliation as he bellowed, "You made me play by your rules for years and then some guy comes along, and you want to drop me like a bad habit? I divorced her for you, and you just move forward with your life like I didn't mean anything to you? It doesn't work like that, Rain!"

"Capri, be quiet!"

He ignored her. "Who is Jhalil? Huh?" He looked at the text messages. "I see you've sent naked pictures to him, so obviously he's been smashing too. You're nothing but a little whore."

Lorraina scrambled to her feet and tried to grab her phone, but he was much quicker, taller, and driven by emotions. Embarrassment caused warm tears to spring to her eyes.

"Lower your voice!" she hissed.

"Answer me! WHO IS HE?"

"Hey, hey!" a worker from the deli department stepped over to see if everything was okay. "What's going on? Sir, you need to calm down and step away from this young lady NOW! Ma'am, are you okay?"

"This doesn't concern you!" Capri yelled.

The employee, who appeared to be a manager by his different uniform, bent to pick up the fallen food and help Lorraina gain some sort of control and dignity. "It's my business when one of my customers are in harm's way. You need to leave this store right away!"

Other patrons inched closer and listened in. Lorraina ducked her head ashamedly and decided that she could wait another day to shop for groceries. Capri had shocked her with his behavior. Not once in the time that she knew him, had he ever become this violent, aggressive, or demeaning. Frankly, it terrified her.

"Just great, Lorraina. You have everybody fooled and thinking you're this angel," Capri chuckled painfully, tossing her phone back to her. He rammed the cart into a wall, and then stalked off. When he spoke again, he looked back at the employee, saying, "You're taking up for a woman who feels it's okay to sleep around and play with people's heart until it's time to move onto the next. Go to hell, Lorraina!"

"Ma'am, are you sure you're okay?"

Lorraina nodded to the question, kept her head low, and shrugged her purse strap over her shoulder. She whispered an apology as she walked past the worker and then literally ran towards her car. Not once did she see the young lady, who was watching the entire scene unfold, standing next to the bank that was attached to the grocery store. Lorraina was so distraught that she did not observe the young lady who was shocked, crying, and red in the face with dejection and disbelief.

Lorraina did not ever notice Kylie standing just a few feet away.

Chapter Seven

Jhalil Harrison was in the zone as he pounded the pavement mile after mile. The briskness of the morning was perfect as he jogged with his headphones on. The semi-new running shoes bounced off the sidewalk, while his matching compression joggers conformed to his body as perspiration left his pores. He breathed out of his mouth to soothe his erratic breathing. Sweat had long ago formed along his hairline and collected in the material of his compression tank top.

He checked his watch. Jhalil had run a total of three miles, completing his two-hour workout. He had a clearer mind, and a more refreshed outlook on the day. What had started out as a bad morning had now turned into a better day; all he needed now was something to feed his muscles.

His eyes scanned the area and zeroed in on the Starbucks on the corner. He jogged over, ordered a few things, and then settled in a booth near the window. As he waited for his name to be called, he looked down at his aching knuckles and shook his head. He still could not believe what had taken place just an hour and a half ago, during his boxing session.

"Are these your gloves?"

Jhalil looked up from stretching on the floor. A guy stood over him, outfitted similarly in workout clothing, and held up a pair of boxing gloves. They were red; Jhalil's set was blue.

"No. I'm not sure whose gloves those are," he said, and then went back to doing lunges.

"Oh okay," the guy said, and then motioned towards the boxing ring. "You come here often?"

"Every week."

59

"Cool, and are you one of the paid professionals?"

Jhalil sighed and realized that his quiet time was now interrupted. "No, I compete every month for charity."

The stranger nodded with approval. "Nice, bro. Can you spar with me? My partner left while we were warming up."

"That's fine," Jhalil gave in.

He was always kind to others and knew that the guy wasn't doing any harm by wanting to warm up. Jhalil could use a few extra minutes of cardio anyway. He stood, shoved his mouth guard in, strapped on his gloves securely, and then turned to the stranger. "What's your name, bro?"

"Capri."

"Jhalil. Let's do it." They bumped gloves.

Jhalil followed behind the slightly slimmer and shorter man, and could not recall why the name sounded so familiar. He figured that they had crossed paths before and knew that the old saying was true; it was a small world.

They entered the boxing ring designated strictly for practicing and warming up. A few other guys were standing around talking, jumping rope, and looking on casually. Jhalil and Capri bounced around on their tiptoes, positioned their arms upward, and then threw jabs out in front of each other. All bystanders could hear their patterned breathing.

To Jhalil's surprise, Capri began to talk.

"You married, bro?"

"Nah. You?" he asked breathily and ducked his head from Capri's incoming jab.

"Recently divorced the woman of my dreams," Capri explained in between panting.

"Oh yeah? If you don't mind me asking, why the divorce route, if she was the woman of your dreams?"

Capri paused for a second, looked down at his gloved fists, and then spit out saliva. He went back to bouncing around on his tiptoes. "She was the woman of my dreams, but I wasn't in love with her."

60

"Oh," Jhalil said simply and wondered why this stranger was telling him his life story. Many men entered the boxing ring to relieve stress and get a good workout in, but it was never to reveal personal details like how Capri was doing.

"Yeah, I divorced her, thinking I would marry my mistress and live happily ever after," he continued to talk, and then punched Jhalil in his shoulder. "But she told me that she had already fallen in love with some other man."

Jhalil took a step back and looked down at the area where he had been punched. "You good?"

Capri raised his hands and apologized. "My mistake, bro. I miscalculated my distance."

The two men continued to bounce around and throw jabs, and Capri continued to speak painfully about his estranged lover.

"She was everything I wanted. Perfect body, sweet personality, incredible mind, and a smile that could light up any room," Capri exclaimed with a sparkle in his eye. As he focused back on Jhalil, his eyes seemed to darken to a midnight black. "Even her name was beautiful. Lorraina."

Jhalil stopped what he was doing and looked at Capri. For the longest time, they stared each other down, and then Jhalil took a wild guess. "Wait a minute. Do we know each other?"

"Nah, but you seem to know my woman. She was supposed to be with me!" Capri unstrapped his gloves and then threw them to the floor. "I came here to tell you to stay away from Lorraina. I'm the only man that should be touching her body and stimulating her mind, you hear me?"

"Aye, you're trippin', my dude!" Jhalil warned and removed his own boxing gloves. He tossed them to the floor and stepped towards Capri. Their breathing was still uneven, and a crowd seemed to have formed around them. "That's not your woman. She can make her own decisions and if seeing me is one of them, then that's HER choice."

"What did I say, bruh?" Capri pushed Jhalil. "We've been messin' around for the last few years. You're just somebody she sees occasionally to pass the time."

"First off." Jhalil pushed him back. "Stop calling me 'bro' like you know me. Two, obviously, she doesn't want YOU, if she's in my bed every night. You may have had her body for a few years, but I've had her heart for the last month."

Capri's eyes widened in shock, as Jhalil continued to push his buttons. He stepped closer to Capri and whispered, "Now that we all know who's the better man here, maybe you should patch things up with wifey, and leave Lorraina's panties to me. Time to let that fantasy go, 'cause you sound mad crazy…bro."

As if gasoline was poured and a burning matchstick was thrown on top of it, the two men exploded in a war of words, punches, and fighting. Instead of breaking up the scuffle, surrounding men video recorded the fight, and seemed to think that this was another round of sparring warm-ups. The owner of the boxing club quickly emerged with two armed security guards, and yelled for them to stop.

When Jhalil and Capri continued to brawl and curse one another out, the security guards jumped into the ring, and physically separated them. "Enough, you two! What's going on? This is a place of peace!"

"Donald, you know me and what I stand for," Jhalil bellowed.

His knuckles were bloodied and raw while his arms were sore from pummeling Capri's lean body. He shrugged out of the guard's arms, dusting himself off, and spitting off to the side of the ring. His eyes were fiery.

"I'm one of the coolest cats you know! This cornball over here disrespected me first."

"Whatever beef y'all have, keep it on the streets. This is MY club, and inside, I want unity. There's enough killin' and hatin' going around. Why are you fighting in the first *place?" Donald screamed, looking back and forth between the two men. Then, he turned to Capri. "Listen, there are no hard feelings, but I've never seen you around here before, so I'm going to have to ask you to please leave my club."*

"Whatever. But this ain't over, Jhalil," Capri called as he was escorted out. "Stay away from Lorraina!"

"Get you some help, man," Jhalil said and waved him off. He was unbothered and far from worried. Obviously, the man had some serious issues. Capri had given him nothing but a headache, and he was without any blemishes other than his raw knuckles. He planned to talk to Lorraina sometime this evening about her ex-lover.

Jhalil's thoughts were interrupted when his name was called by a cute barista with a chocolate complexion. He noticed that she drew a heart underneath his name. He smiled absently, knowing he would do five to ten years in jail because she was no older than 17. He headed back to his seat and whipped out his iPhone. He had to meet up with Lorraina as soon as possible, though he wasn't ready to do the unthinkable.

Her baggage was getting out of hand.

He called her once, then twice, and then sent a text message. She was probably busy, so in the meantime, he had to get himself together. He knew that this was not the life he wanted to lead. Lately, even before he had run into Lorraina that night at the restaurant, he had begun to feel guilty. He was feeling useless, and smoking, drinking, and having sex was becoming a regular occurrence that just didn't fulfill him anymore.

He certainly had not been taught those ways and wondered where it all went south for him. Besides working as a director at a digital marketing agency, turning up in a local club seemed to be where he spent all his time now. Drowning himself in liquor and women was only to fill a void; it was the void that he knew only one person could fill.

Jesus Christ.

Jhalil's parents raised him to be a God-fearing young man and most of his life, he was a regular on their community's church scene. You could find Jhalil in the tenor section of the choir, volunteering at youth night, and drumming every week at Bible Study. He loved God, then and now. But as an adult, he had become so frustrated with the church and its emotionally driven people. There were so many disappointments and letdowns in the clergy that he figured no church was right for him.

When he met Lorraina, his assumptions had been proven correctly. Here she was, a pastor and self-proclaimed woman of God, yet she dressed, fornicated, and drank like a heathen. Where was the standard? She was sexy and interesting, but she was holding him back. Not to mention, he had broken things off with his woman, Y'landa, who was much more wholesome. He needed to get right with God again, and if it meant saying goodbye to her, then so be it.

After all, she never told him that she loved him when he said it.

Chapter Eight

Lorraina was facedown in her pillows, naked, and dripping with moisture. She had a male companion on top of her when Jhalil's call came through. Her eyes cut over to the vibrating phone, and then she threw it across the room. Behind her, showing her all kinds of love, sensuality, and roughness was one of the deacons from her church; his name was Donnell. He had been eyeing her for a while and since she and Jhalil were on a "break," she had reached out to Donnell to get her evening fix. He was a clumsy lover, but it would hold her over until she found someone else.

Donnell collapsed beside her suddenly and Lorraina was confused. "Wait. You're *done?*"

She assumed he was ready to switch positions, not take a nap.

"Yeah. That was good, huh?" he breathed huskily, wiping his forehead with the back of his hand. He ran his other hand across his chest.

Lorraina continued to watch him under the curve of her eyelashes. Then she shook her head.

"Please leave."

"Why? I thought we were having a good time."

"Because I said so. You've been here for over 30 minutes."

"And?"

"Don't you have to get back to work?" Lorraina stood up, completely naked, and walked to the bathroom. She placed her foot on top of her phone and kicked it in front of her. She bent to pick it up when it was far out of Donnell's line of vision.

"Who was that anyway?"

She paused, turned to smile at him charmingly, and then shrugged. "Telemarketer."

Donnell grew quiet and relaxed into the pillows. As Lorraina cleaned up, she could hear him moving around and wondered what he was up to. She freshened up, threw on a pair of jeans, and then clasped her bra.

He was now fully clothed and held his workbag under an arm. "Are you screwin' him too?"

"Excuse me?" Lorraina paused as she shoved an arm into the sleeve of her blouse. Her heart skipped a beat as he motioned towards the phone sticking from her front pocket.

"Whoever Jhalil is. I saw his name pop up on the screen before you threw it," Donnell explained, while tightening his jaw. "Are you sleepin' with him too?"

"Why...why do you ask?"

"Why...why else would I be asking?" he mocked her as she stuttered. "You said you had eyes for *me*. I already knew about Capri, but why are you sleepin' with other people? Do you know how that makes you look?"

Lorraina looked at him incredulously and continued to button her blouse. "I should be asking you that same thing. You're engaged with a child on the way. I'm single with no ring on my finger. I can do whatever I want, and I NEVER said I had eyes for you. Don't flatter yourself."

"Yeah, okay," Donnell chuckled and put the strap of his bag over a shoulder. He eyed her with disbelief. "Goodbye, Pastor."

"Goodbye, one-minute man," she called out, as he stuck his middle finger up at her, "I mean, *Deacon*."

He slammed the door, and then she heard his tires burning rubber, minutes later, as he drove off angrily. She could not believe his audacity or his comments. Their talk had been clear; they discussed that what happened between the sheets stayed between the sheets. She vowed that she would not treat him any differently while at church. He seemed to agree and understand her rules, but now he wanted to insult and degrade her.

That was her first and last escapade with Donnell.

As she calmed down, her thoughts went back to Jhalil. As much as she longed to speak with him, she was also avoiding his calls. She had been the first to establish a no strings attached mindset. But she could not help but to think that somewhere along the way, between kissing and touching this incredible man, her heart was now involved.

He was no longer just a fun time for her. He was slowly becoming a constant in her life, but she didn't want to fall for him. She didn't want to love him. Still, every day, she found herself craving his one-of-a-kind humor, warm hugs, and sexy reassurance. This time apart had almost broken her because she absolutely missed him.

He was the complete package, but he SCARED her. She was afraid of how vulnerable she was with him, and what it all meant. In just a short time she had trusted him with her life and body, and yet she had succumbed to temptation and slept with another man. Even as she had done the forgettable deed, her mind had been on Jhalil.

Blowing out a deep breath, she decided to call him back.

He answered on the first ring. "We need to talk."

"Hey, to you too," Lorraina said. "What's wrong?"

Jhalil ignored her panicked question and sighed into the phone. "I need to see you right away. Are you free?"

They made plans to meet up within the hour at Jhalil's place.

Lorraina decided that she was going to be real with herself and be real with Jhalil. She changed clothes now that she knew she would be seeing him and decided to wear a maxi dress that hugged her hips and dipped low to show a little cleavage.

She sprayed on the perfume that he mentioned he liked on her, and then pinned her hair up into a messy bun. With her pinky fingers, she pulled out a few wisps of hair to frame her face. Jhalil loved when she wore her nude lipstick and applied that to her mouth before deeming her appearance as perfect as it would get.

She made it to Jhalil's house in record time, checked herself in the mirror to be sure her makeup was still flawless, and then exhaled deeply. It was now or never.

He greeted her at the door with a hug and a kiss on the temple.

"Hey, honey," she whispered to him.

He answered the door in just a towel and his Adidas flip-flops. Lorraina cursed silently, knowing it was the last thing that she wanted to see. She needed a clear mind, but here he was, showing his imprint and damp chest. She could see traces of bruising on his skin but decided not to ask about it. It would only cause her to stare longer.

"How are you? You've got to excuse me. I just hopped out of the shower."

68

"No, uh…no worries." She grinned and gave him another half-hug. "I really missed you."

"I missed you too. A lot more than I care to admit."

He ran to put some clothes on and then returned to her shortly. She had settled in one of his coffee brown couches and was distractedly watching a rerun of some sketch comedy show.

"So, what's up? You've been on my mind heavy lately," Lorraina admitted.

Jhalil sat on the arm of his couch and took Lorraina's hand. His eyes were bloodshot, and he slurred slightly when he began to talk. "Likewise, likewise. That's why I've been blowing up your phone all day. I'm going to be honest with you. I just need you to please listen for now."

"Okay."

Jhalil sighed and then stood up. He began to pace as he shared his deepest, most intimate thoughts. "I don't know when it happened. I was just trying to have a good time with you. I saw you ridin' that bull that night, and you were honestly the most attractive woman I had EVER seen in my life. Still are. I mean, *look* at you."

Lorraina blushed and gnawed on the inside of her cheek.

"We had some of the best sex in my life. I became addicted to you in a short time, and it tripped me out, because I'm *never* thrown off my game by anybody. I'm one of the senior partners at my company; I meet with executives and millionaires on a daily," Jhalil said. He smiled and seemed to look deep into her soul. "No one has *ever* impacted my life the way that you have, and I can't believe these words are even leavin' my mouth, ma."

Lorraina swallowed hard and was unsure where this conversation was going, but she knew that she would tell him how she was feeling. It was only right.

"I fell for you, shorty. I fell *in* love with you. You can't even imagine how hard not seeing you has been for me. I felt like an addict."

Lorraina could relate more than he realized.

"But," he continued faintly, "Sometimes even when things feel like they're going perfectly, it still doesn't make it right. It still doesn't mean two people are meant to be together."

Just like that, her heart dropped.

"I ran into one of your exes, or whatever you want to call him, today. Capri."

Lorraina swallowed hard. He studied her for a moment.

"He told me he loves you, and that he wants to be with you and all that jazz. I didn't care because I know whose bed you were sleeping in just about every night." He moved his hands as he attempted to express himself. "But what put it all into perspective for me was the fact that this cat was willin' to fight over you. Well, we *did* exchange blows and words. That's why my body's black and blue now. He threatened my life over you. Obviously, there's more to this story, and for that reason, I have to remove myself from this situation."

"Jhalil…"

"Let me finish. Now, I'm not trying to break your heart, make you cry, or upset you in any way. But I think it's really messed up that I was honest from the jump, told you about my woman, and then broke up with her for you. I thought we could sort of work towards a relationship. But you never once mentioned that you and Capri had something going on. On top of that, he said that he divorced his wife over you. I'm not sure I'm what you need."

Lorraina attempted to speak, but Jhalil put his hand up.

"I'm still not done talking! Like I said, I was beginning to feel something for you. Even now as I look at you, I'm struggling to keep my eyes off your body, and I'm fighting the urge to take you in the room and make love to you. I can't understand how you still have that effect on me. But I can't continue to go against God's purpose for my life and be distracted, especially over a woman who has more skeletons in her closet than she bothered to share."

Jhalil grew quiet and Lorraina decided that it was her turn to finally speak.

"You're not going to do this right now. You are not going to blame me for another man's OBSESSION with me, and his reaction to an affair. I can't help that he fell in love with me and that he tracked you down or fought you. I'm sorry it happened, but Jhalil, don't punish me for Capri's actions. I care for you!"

"You *care* for me?" he chuckled and moved to sit on the couch. "Nah, you care about how I make you feel. That's why you only call me when you need to clear your mind or if you're stressed. Lorraina, you ignored 90 percent of my calls today. You only came because you assumed I wanted to do something other than talk. I know game when I see it."

Lorraina spoke over him, "I let you talk, so let me talk. Baby, I never expected that we would be anything more than friends. We went into this with the intentions to just have fun. Our lovemaking turned into love, and you can't deny that. You said so yourself the last time we had sex!"

71

"That was just pillow talk," he admitted, but it was obvious he was lying.

Lorraina chuckled painfully, "So you lied about that? Yeah, okay. Why the sudden change? Why are you acting like this?"

"I should have never taken this thing further than a 'hi' and 'bye' in the parking lot that night. I should have never fooled around with a *pastor* at that. Now, the love of my life's gone, and I'm involved with a woman who has more sex partners than the members of her church."

It was as if Mike Tyson had punched her. Lorraina could feel the life literally being sucked out of her with his harsh words. She could feel the drop in her heart and then the slap to the face, as he went on and on about how much he regretted getting closer to her.

Then, like a rubber band being stretched to its maximum capacity, she snapped. "How can you say that to me? I love you...I fell in *LOVE* with YOU!" Her balled fists came up to connect with Jhalil's face, his chest, and his arms.

He stood unmoving, taking blow after blow from her.

"If you felt this way, why did you sleep with me? Why did you even come up to talk to me? You talk about my shortcomings, but you're just as bad!"

Lorraina continued to hit on him until he had no choice but to wrap both arms around her forearms and slam her down onto his bed. It was not forceful, but it got her attention. With her arms bound, Lorraina began to weep into the crook of his neck.

Jhalil fought back tears as he continued to hold her hostage in his embrace.

"How could you say that?" she sobbed. "You don't even realize how much I love you. I don't like Capri in that way, and never did. It was only sex—nothing more! I love you...I want YOU! Please...don't leave me. Don't do this."

Jhalil held her until she literally cried herself to sleep. Only then did he let her go.

Chapter Nine

Lorraina woke up when a cold towel was rubbed against the side of her face. She shook her head quickly in shock, gasped, and then breathed a sigh of relief when she saw that it was Jhalil standing above her. He had a look of concern on his handsome face.

Lorraina rubbed her eyes and sat up further on the earth-tone furniture. Before he could speak, another woman entered the room wearing floral pants and an off-the-shoulder blouse. She was well put together with an air of class about her, and some may have even called her conservative. For Lorraina, she was confused as to why another person was in their space.

"Who are you?" Lorraina asked and then looked to Jhalil.

The woman's perfectly arched eyebrows flew up. "Jhalil knows exactly who I am, sweetheart. Who are *you*?"

"What are you, a parrot? I asked first!"

"Aye, aye, stop it," Jhalil interrupted before an argument could take place. "Lorraina, this is Y'landa, the girlfriend I was telling you about. Baby, this is Lorraina. You both know about each other from what I've told you, but now, you each have a face with the name."

"Why am I here, Jhalil? What games are you playing?" Y'landa asked in irritation. She rolled her eyes as she looked back over to Lorraina. "You could've done this over the phone."

"Done *what* over the phone?" Lorraina asked and returned her stare. They were both acting weird, and the tension was so thick in the room that one could have literally cut it with a knife. "*Jhalil?*"

He looked fearful to say his next words. But then he took a deep breath, gulped loudly, and then looked Lorraina in the eyes.

"Sweetheart, I've pretty much already told you where I stand, but I just wanted to apologize to the both of you face to face. Y'landa, I'm sorry for taking you through this rollercoaster of breaking up then making up. Lorraina, I'm sorry for leading you on. I should have never pursued anything with you," Jhalil admitted.

Y'landa looked excited that he was giving their relationship a second chance while Lorraina fought the urge to damage the lamp on his nightstand. She had to admit, they *did* make a beautiful couple, but she would have much rather been on Jhalil's arm.

"I respect your decision. I was better off without you anyway," Lorraina declared. She kept her head high, smoothed out her clothing as she stood, and then made her way towards the door.

Jhalil followed her while Y'landa settled on the loveseat. "Can I at least walk you out?"

"No, thank you. You've done enough," Lorraina told him. As she swung the short strap of her purse onto her shoulder, she looked him in the eye. "Know this. Years from now, you'll miss the way I smelled, the way I tasted, and the way I made you feel."

"Yeah, I know. I already do," he admitted, "but that still doesn't change my mind." He rubbed his neatly trimmed goatee and mumbled, "Take care, shorty."

She knew that his eyes were on her backside as she made her way down the steps and across the pavement. She gave an extra twist of her hips to give him one final show.

Lorraina held her tears at bay as she sped off in her truck and drove above the speed limit to her home. Only then did she cry. Everything that was of value in her place was shattered, broken, and destroyed with the anger overtaking her senses.

"How DARE you break things off with me! How DARE you hurt me like this!" she cried.

With her arm, she flung vases to the floor, punched the walls, and kicked the legs of her table until they cracked.

The ruckus she made was loud and alarming, and soon, there was a knock at her door. Lorraina ignored who she assumed was a nosey neighbor. The person eventually went away.

Hours later, as she held a wine bottle in one hand, and the remote control in the other hand, she realized the visitor was Khloey. There were over 14 missed calls, 11 unread text messages, and four voicemail messages from her. She ignored them all and sat in the center of the mess she had made.

Her fingers were red and raw, and she knew tomorrow they would be sore and bruised. Warm tears made their way down her face. They were unstoppable and salty as they slid past her lips, over her chin, and down her collarbone. Lorraina's eyes were low with the heaviness of her sleepy eyelids. She needed a good night's rest, but not before she spoke to God.

With bitterness, she slammed the wine bottle to the ground and could not remember ever feeling so empty. She looked towards the ceiling and through her tears and quivering mouth, she cried out.

"Enough! I can't take it anymore! You've taken everything from me. EVERYTHING! God, You've taken my grandma, and You've taken the only man I ever loved. What did I ever do to You? Why can't I just get this right?"

Lorraina stood up with a hiccup. Then she sat back down as dizziness overtook her. The alcohol was taking effect as she hoped it would. Maybe then she wouldn't feel so horrible inside.

"Why...why can't I stop messing up? I've fornicated, lied, and cheated. I've done it all! I'm not perfect, so why did You call me to do this? Why did You appoint me as a pastor? I don't even have my life figured out, but You expect me to help others? This assignment is too hard. It's ruining my life!" she screamed, and her voice seemed to have gotten decibels louder.

Shakily, she pointed her finger to the ceiling, and shook her head. "I give up! I can't do this! It's all Your fault! I don't want to be a pastor anymore."

Lorraina blinked slowly and wrapped herself in a blanket. She let out a hiccup again, as a deep sleep overtook her.

Chapter Ten

"Rain! Get up! It smells like butt and morning breath in here! LUH-RAIN-NUH!"

Lorraina gasped with panic when a cup of water was splashed in her face. She shook her head to gain consciousness and attempted to glare at the concerned face before her. It was Khloey. Lorraina rolled her eyes and settled back in her comfortable position. She was ready to go back to dreamland but felt the coolness of the water seeping further in her clothes.

"Have you washed up today?" her friend asked.

Khloey's index finger and thumb was smashing her nostrils together to block out the unpleasant smell.

"And look at your hair...and this *trash* everywhere. Rain, what did he do to you, honey? What happened?"

Lorraina had literally sat in her same position since the day Jhalil had broken things off with her. It had been three days since her heart broke into a million pieces and three days since her world crumbled. She had only gotten up to use the bathroom, grab another bottle of wine, and eat the slim pickings from her fridge. Her breath was strong and offensive, while her body odor was downright unacceptable. She had walked over the mess she made and had not picked up a single item that she had thrown during her tantrum. This was her house, her body, and her choice to do absolutely nothing.

"How did you get in here?" Lorraina asked without any energy. She did not have the strength to yell or defend her decisions to sulk. Plus, her head throbbed.

"I have a key, remember? You didn't answer my calls, so I came over because everyone thinks you are DEAD! Thank God, you're not, but spiritually and emotionally, you are a wreck. Get up," her friend demanded again.

Lorraina reluctantly stood up with the help of Khloey.

"You've only known this man for some months, and you're acting like *this*? What happened between you two to make you…LOSE it? What did he say to you, or do to you?" Khloey wanted to know.

Lorraina sighed and shook her head. She was all cried out, but her heart seemed to break as she said, "He left me."

"Left you for *what*?"

"I don't want to talk about it." Lorraina pulled leisurely from Khloey's hold and moved towards the kitchen to search for the white Zinfandel bottle. "Did you take my champagne?"

"Rain, that's enough! You've got bottles everywhere. This isn't you! I'm not letting you drink anything else, and I'm not leaving your side until you get yourself together. Come on."

With the help of Khloey, she took a much-needed bubble bath, washed and combed her hair, and ate a regular meal with water. Her home was tidied up and like new within an hour and a half. Khloey sat down to relax for a moment and shook her head in disbelief.

"Look, honey, I know you're going through hard times right now, but I need you to focus. I need you to come back to me and get it together.

You're a pastor and more than anything, you're STRONGER than this."

"Everybody has a breaking moment. Why can't I have mine? Why can't the encourager receive encouragement every once in awhile?" Lorraina challenged.

"Trust me, I get it. But listen. There's so much going on right now, and I wanted you to be the first to know."

"Know what? Khlo, I don't want to hear any more bad news," she said and ate the last of the homemade pancakes. "I can't take anything else."

"You uh…you have no choice, but we're going to face this together," Khloey said and pulled out her phone. She tilted it so that Lorraina could also see the video that was about to play.

Before long, crystal clear footage of Lorraina and Deacon Donnell appeared on the phone screen. She was panting and moaning with her backside to the camera. Donnell, with his pants and underwear hanging around his ankles, was looking back at the camera and seemed aware that it was recording them.

Lorraina could not believe her eyes and squinted to look at the caption written under the video, and the handful of comments that followed. She was called every name in the book, while a few people wasted no time in identifying who she was. She then looked at the social media site that had her images. It was some well-known hip-hop entertainment site that she knew had millions of subscribers.

Her breath caught in her throat at the reality that her naked body had gone viral. She was no longer a hypocrite behind closed doors. Her secrets were now revealed, and they had come to the light in the worst way possible. Everybody and their momma could see her bouncing breasts and jiggling buttocks. She thought of the shocked facial expressions and reactions from her church members, family and friends, and even Jhalil. He would probably never return to her after this fiasco.

Lorraina looked at Khloey, and to her surprise, tears began to form. She figured she had done all of her crying.

"So, what now? What do I do? Those viewers know my name, city, church name…all that. I'm screwed. I am so screwed. Why does this keep happening to me?" she asked, with panic in her voice. "This just can't be real."

"Well, it *is* real, and I'm not going to say that this is an easy fix, BUT you have to let me help you. I'm no publicist or manager but I am your friend and I've got your back. We're going to get through this, you hear? Everything is going to be okay."

Everything was *not* going to be okay, and both she and Lorraina knew it. Within a matter of hours, the world seemed to know "Pastor Lorraina" with the big butt. She received all kinds of calls, text messages, and emails. She even received a few nasty photographs from men around the world who wanted her in their beds next. Lorraina grew sick to her stomach.

As she emptied the contents from her tummy into the toilet, she received another phone call. It was the presiding bishop over her church. She gulped and knew exactly why he was calling at almost three in the morning. Like most people, he had heard the news or seen the video. Lorraina gargled, composed herself, and then called him back. With only a few words, she was reprimanded, scolded, and ridiculed. Her titles were stripped from her, her duties and accolades were revoked, and she was instructed to stay far away from The McCall Worship Center until everything died down.

"That's my family's church!" she protested. She could feel the migraine beginning to plague her. She literally could not take anymore. "You can't take that away from me!"

"Oh, but we can. You see, when one of the minister's sons got ahold of this, we set up an impromptu teleconference and took a vote on whether or not you're fit for this position. You gave us many great years, but your time is up. We had some suspicions that things were not as they seemed, but this takes the cake and there is NO coming back from such a fall. I'm sorry, but…"

Lorraina closed her eyes against the harsh words. "Please. I just…I just need your forgiveness and patience while I…I get myself together. I can make a statement. I can publicly apologize. I—I can—"

The bishop didn't miss a beat. "…You've been replaced, Ms. McCall. Your services as the senior pastor are no longer needed. You'll be in our prayers. Get some help."

Click.

The grumpy old man, who Lorraina never liked to begin with, hung up on her. She screamed out and with Khloey looking on, she threw the phone into the wall with a crash. Her friend jumped in shock but remained silent. Lorraina walked into her bedroom with her friend in tow, and then she collapsed on the bed. She was beginning to think that crying was going to be her favorite activity for the next few days, weeks, or months.

She was not as sad about her ministry credentials being interrogated and taken away, especially after questioning God the way she had. That wasn't the problem. She would eventually get over the shock of going viral and having her naked body splayed for all to see. She had enough confidence to rebuild her brand and restore some dignity. That wasn't the problem either. The biggest disappointment and dejection she felt was that only man that she had ever loved had slipped from her fingers and moved on without her. He would not be with her as she rebuilt her life. He would not be returning to her arms, bed, or life anytime soon...if ever.

That thought absolutely sickened and terrified her.

Chapter Eleven

Six months later...

God had not forsaken Lorraina. Despite the sin that she once basked in everyday, despite the fornication she loved so much, and despite the disobedience of not delivering God's Word as she was called to do, God had not forgotten about her. She cleaned herself up with both professional help and the support of friends and family. As much as she loved and missed Jhalil, she had tucked away their sweet and brief memories, and moved on with her head as high as her heels.

Though the video of her sexual affairs was devastating when it first went viral, her "fame" didn't last any more than two weeks, before the next viral video took over the internet and adverted everyone's attention. Still, since then, Lorraina had dedicated to living a celibate, quiet life.

She no longer wanted to work at the forefront of a ministry, so she chose to attend a mega church where she could blend in and be "normal" for once. She would not have to preach or serve in any capacity. Instead, she would literally go to church, sing her praises to God, and then have the freedom to go back home without overwhelming obligations or responsibilities. Just yesterday, she had completed her final Sexaholics Anonymous meeting. She had met many new friends and she felt refreshed and renewed.

She was not alone in this fight and could move forward with her life without any more restrictions. It felt good.

The speaking engagement that she had booked so many months ago rolled around and it was time to prepare for her speech. She had written four mini self-help books about her life's experiences and was going to be talking with women on how to overcome depression, low self-esteem, addiction, and other adversities that she had also faced.

This conference was supposed to be laidback, life changing, and fun, so she chose to wear a slim-fitting, olive-colored bodycon dress. It had a lace, mock neck, and touched the tops of her knees. She paired the dress with strappy, nude-colored heels. Her hair, which was French braided to the back of her head neatly, was adorned with gold-tone beads. Her makeup was natural and light, and her eyes sparkled more than usual.

She looked youthful, fresh, and ready for the world.

As she made her way to the venue, she went over her speech in her head and bit down on her lip so much that she was sure that her lipstick was smudged.

"You've got this, Rain. You've got this," she assured herself.

Hundreds of women were in attendance tonight—some broken and widowed, and others newly married or single. One thing that they had in common is they were all looking for a word of hope and she prayed that God would give her the right message to bring.

When it was time for her to go up onstage an hour and a half later, she was prayed up, and was as prepared as she could possibly be. Her nerves had become butterflies in the pit of her stomach, and her palms felt clammy.

"God, be with me," she prayed softly.

"Ms. McCall?" another voice broke through the silence of the waiting room and interrupted her erratic thoughts. "We're ready for you on stage three."

"Okay." Lorraina nodded.

She followed behind the young woman, who was most likely an intern. She had a headset on and a clipboard in her hands as she spoke into a microphone. "Testing, one, two, three. Testing, one, two. You're all set with this mic. Did you need a bottled water as well onstage?"

"No, thank you. I have my own," Lorraina politely declined. She took a sip of the lukewarm beverage in question and exhaled deeply. "All those women came out for *me*?"

"They sure did. You must be an awesome speaker."

"I do okay," Lorraina said humbly. "I just pray it goes over well."

"It will. I have complete faith in you," the woman assured her and patted her shoulder. "Knock 'em dead, Ms. McCall."

Lorraina smiled and waved a goodbye as the intern walked off to tend to something else. Lorraina took another deep breath and knew it had to be her twentieth time or so. It was time to go up, so she clutched her microphone a little tighter, straightened out the material of her dress, and stepped up the stairs one at a time.

"Ladies, please welcome tonight's keynote speaker, Ms. Lorraina McCall."

To a generous round of applause, Lorraina smiled and entered the stage from the side. She exhaled one final time, waved her hand towards the sea of women, and then put the microphone just below her bottom lip.

"Good evening, ladies. How are y'all doing?"

"Good!" a few people shouted, while others clapped and nodded their responses.

Lorraina smiled, sat on the stool that had already been set out for her, and then carefully worked the microphone into its stand.

"I'm so honored to be here at the Empowering Women's Conference. As the beautiful emcee introduced me, I'm Lorraina McCall. I was skeptical about coming here tonight for a number of reasons. Most of all, I was nervous that my life wouldn't reflect what the conference embodies; poise, grace, holiness, and redemption."

Lorraina looked out to the right side of the stage and crossed her leg. She continued to speak candidly.

"But then I began to think about Moses' life, and how God used him in a mighty way, even after he murdered someone. I thought about how God used Abraham although he lied repeatedly. I even thought about how God turned things around for Noah, despite his drunkenness. Honestly, I realized that my sins and my shortcomings weren't so bad, and that if God could use those people in the Bible, He could certainly use *me*."

"Okay now!" someone yelled in support.

Lorraina chuckled at the woman and held up her hand. "Don't get me preachin' in here. I didn't come for that. Instead, I just wanted to share a few words that may encourage you. I want to meet you exactly where you are in this time of your life. Can I uplift and inspire you all today? Is that all right?"

"That's all right!" another woman cried out and the remainder of the audience seemed to agree as they clapped, whistled, and cheered.

"That's all right. You can encourage us…as long as you promise not to sleep with any of our men afterward!"

Lorraina's smile faded at the words. The voice was oddly familiar, but she had no idea where it stemmed from with so many people staring back at her.

"Excuse me?" Lorraina asked.

"You heard me, HOMEWRECKER!"

The front of the audience gasped. They were probably the only people in the venue who could hear the accusatory statements. Lorraina squinted and looked down towards the only woman standing up in the crowd. She wore a red wig, with dark sunglasses perched on the bridge of her nose. She also wore black, homely clothing.

"Excuse me?" Lorraina repeated.

In all her years of public speaking, she had been trained to ignore hecklers or distractions. However, there was no way she was going to let someone come in and steal her shine on a night like tonight.

This was supposed to be *Lorraina's* moment.

She could feel her heart begin to beat faster to the point it felt her chest would explode. Her eyes searched for the woman's features, but they were masked by the shades and ugly, lengthy wig.

"You're such a hypocrite," the woman continued and made her way out into the aisle of the auditorium. "You don't care about other people. You only live life to satisfy and please yourself, even if it's at the expense of other people's happiness. You don't read the Bible! You don't respect other people's marriages! You lie, fornicate, curse, and sleep with married men! So, why in the WORLD are you speaking to us at a women's

88

empowerment conference when you know NOTHING about that?"

Security rushed out from the side of the stage and headed towards the troublemaker. The crowd grew rowdy with confusion and shock. Whispers and murmurs became louder as the drama unfolded. Before security could reach the unknown woman, Lorraina watched in horror as she dug around in her oversized bag and pulled a gun out.

The women who were closest to the perpetrator screamed and chaos ensued. People jumped out of their seats, pushed others, and ran to take cover. The woman, who had interrupted her speech, took things a step further and aimed the gun towards Lorraina. The unarmed security guards slowed down and then raised their arms cautiously, trying to access the situation.

The woman did not focus on the beefy men, however. She was looking directly at Lorraina, who had become frozen in place. Tears began to fall from the woman's eyes from what Lorraina could see from the stage. She squinted to look beyond the lights as the woman reached up and took the sunglasses from her saddened eyes. Lorraina gasped.

It was Kylie.

"You *ruined* my marriage! My husband divorced me because he said he was in LOVE with you! How could you? We trusted you with our lives, our spiritual journeys, and our marriage. We let you in on our deepest and darkest secrets. You allowed me, time and time again, to CRY on your shoulder about the same man you were SLEEPING with! How could you betray me this way?" Kylie screamed.

Her fingers shook uncontrollably on the trigger of the gun. Lorraina was still frozen in shock, standing in front of the wooden stool. She wanted to move but every muscle seemed deadened, like she was stuck in quicksand. She wanted to say something, but her throat had closed on her. Even her breaths were shallow and still. She prayed silently that God would touch Kylie's heart and mind to put the gun down.

"Do you know how that feels? Do you know how hard it hurts to try for years to please your husband, look pretty for your husband, or cook and clean for your husband, while he cheats with another woman? A pastor at that? What kind of monster are you?" Kylie continued and walked towards her.

"Kylie, *please* don't do this," Lorraina spoke finally. "I'm so sorry."

"You're sorry? You're *SORRY*?" Kylie looked crazed as she shook her head and put the glasses back over her enraged eyes. Her eyes never left Lorraina's, as she pointed the gun towards the ceiling and let off a shot. This caused more confusion and more disorder, as people scrambled to save themselves. "Oh, you're sorry all right. That's all you can say, huh? You broke up a happy family! It's all your fault that my husband hates me!"

All around them, conference staff and attendees had run off in different directions, including the unarmed security team. People were falling over each other and scrambling to save themselves. There was screaming, crying, and a melee of terrified women. As much as Lorraina wanted to run and protect herself from this madwoman, she knew she had to face her former armor-bearer and friend. Kylie deserved to know how sorry she was.

"Look, honey…"

"Don't call me that! Capri used to call me that!"

Lorraina jumped as Kylie shot a bullet up into the atmosphere once more. She spoke gently and carefully, "I promise you. God has dealt with me, and He's taken EVERYTHING from me. I've lost it all. My pastoral credentials and church were taken away; most of my family won't speak to me, and I'm lonely! My boyfriend left me. I know it doesn't compare to what you went through, but I've learned my lesson! I am so sorry for hurting you, Kylie."

"No, you're not! You think this apology will make everything better? How could you do this to my family? We LOVED and TRUSTED you, Lorraina! You promised to help our marriage, but you ruined it! You ruined my life! You ruined EVERYTHING!" Kylie repeated the phrase that killed Lorraina more and more.

As the trigger was pulled again, Lorraina could not react quickly enough. She watched as Kylie ran towards her and fired again and again. Miraculously, Lorraina was not hit, but she stumbled on the wooden stool, and fell. Kylie took the steps two at a time and caught up to her as she crawled on the floor.

Pow!

Lorraina's hip was hit with a bullet and her flesh burned from the impact.

"Come back here, you homewrecker! I hate you!"

As Kylie raised the gun a final time, Lorraina's life flashed before her eyes. She realized her years of creeping and sinning were not worth it. She pleaded with her eyes to get Kylie to put down the weapon, but it was obvious, that she was far-gone. Kylie snatched off her wig, threw her sunglasses to the ground, and then fell to her knees before Lorraina.

"You know what's crazy? I can't even be mad at you anymore. What's even crazier than that," Kylie chuckled bitterly, "is that I forgive you. What I *do* want you to know is how much you hurt me," Kylie added, seconds before slamming the gun into the side of Lorraina's head.

Lorraina dropped to the stage with a shriek.

"But I'm not God, and I won't judge you— nor will I end your life like I wanted to. You've been through enough and you've learned your lesson, I guess."

Lorraina pressed her hand to her temple where blood oozed below her fingertips. She coughed and attempted to speak, "You didn't deserve this. I—I'm so sorry! I swear!"

Kylie shook her head in defeat. She sat the gun down in front of her and dropped her head in her open palms. She began to cry as Lorraina looked on in shock, unsure what to do or say next. Was Kylie for real? Was this a plot to shoot and kill her? Lorraina's thought were erratic as she pushed the gun out of Kylie's reach, and then scooted closer. Reluctantly, she grabbed Kylie's trembling hands in her bloodied ones.

"I know I'm not perfect and won't ever be perfect. But please believe me when I say God's perfect LOVE and forgiveness is so good. What I did was horrible, and I understand your frustrations and anger, but don't hurt yourself by trying to prove a point," Lorraina said. "I've been humbled, knocked down, and stripped of everything over the last few months. Please know that it was never my intention to hurt you or break up your marriage. I was sick but God healed me from my sex addiction. Please believe me!"

Kylie nodded as she continued to look down. "I know, I know! What was I thinking bringing this gun in here? Oh, my goodness! What's happening to me? I could've killed you or anyone else!"

"Shhh," Lorraina shushed her, and pulled Kylie into her arms in a hug. "Let it go. You didn't kill or hurt anyone, and that's all that matters."

"You're bleeding though!" Kylie panicked. "Oh, my goodness! What did I do? I'm a MONSTER!"

"I'm okay, Kylie. Look at me. I'm alright. I deserved that. Listen, I love you and I promise I will make this right," Lorraina vowed. "We're going to find Capri and bring you two back together. You hear me?"

Kylie nodded and a single tear fell from her eye.

"We're going to both get the help we need, okay?" Lorraina coaxed. "I'm not leaving your side until we do, I promise."

Kylie nodded again. "What have I doooone?" she cried.

"*Freeze!* Put your hands where we can see them!" Behind the women, two police officers rushed in from the entryway, and pointed their guns to where they were huddled together. "Ma'am, drop your weapon!"

"I don't have a weapon," Kylie assured the officers and began to stand up. "See? It's only my…"

She held out her hand to show the officers that her folded sunglasses were in her hand. The policemen became confused and assumed that she held a gun or some sort of weapon and shot bullet after bullet in their direction. A scream ripped from Kylie's lips as she was hit. Her petite frame shook and moved around violently as bullets pierced her body.

"Nooooo!" Lorraina screamed until her voice gave out. "Stop shooting! Stop shooting! She's unarmed!"

The officers reluctantly put their guns down, but it was much too late. Lorraina witnessed in pure terror as Kylie stumbled a few feet, and then fell down with her face up. Two tears, one on each side, rolled down her face as she took her final breath.

Lorraina scrambled on the floor to hold her now deceased friend's body tightly, cried out to the officers for their costly mistakes, and then rocked Kylie back and forth.

"It's all my fault. I'm so sorry!" she sobbed and kissed the only spot of Kylie's face that was free of blood.

"How could I be so stupid? I'm sorry for my mistakes. I'm sorry for causing you pain. You were so loyal, and I didn't tell you enough how much I appreciate you. I'm sorry for all my sins that trickled into your life, baby girl. Please wake up, Ky-Ky. Please, hold on for me. Please, look at me so we can figure out how to move past this. *Please*. Wake up!"

Kylie never woke up.

Chapter Twelve

The police lights and shrill of the sirens, questioning from investigators and medical personnel, flashes from detectives' cameras, and the sounds of crying family members and bystanders were too much for Lorraina to handle. On a gurney, Kylie's body was rolled out. It was completely engulfed in a dark green body bag. As the medics hit a crack in the cement, one of Kylie's petite hands fell out of the bag and hung limply off the gurney. The guilt that Lorraina felt, coupled with the disgust of seeing her friend lifeless all over again, caused her to regurgitate near the curb where an ambulance was parked.

"Ma'am, please allow us to take you to get stitched up," a young paramedic said.

The woman was in her distinctive blue uniform with a stethoscope around her neck. She was also the same woman who checked Kylie's vitals and who had declared that she was dead— although Lorraina already knew the truth. The woman's uniform was covered in dark, crimson blood. *Kylie's* blood.

It made Lorraina sick to her stomach.

"No, just let me die," she said softly. She yanked her wrist from the woman's hold and then began to walk in the opposite direction.

"Ma'am! You have to stay on the scene!" another voice ordered.

One of Lorraina's heels was broken and her dress was ripped and covered in blood. She waved her hand in dismissal at the people calling out to her. She could not care less about any more question and answer sessions. Her friend was dead, and it was all her fault. She felt helpless and she, too, felt lifeless. Just as sure as she felt like she had gotten her life on track, she was taking ten more steps back.

Lorraina stumbled along the pavement for many blocks. She ignored the looks of people passing by and cars driving back and forth. Fat tears rolled down her face and puddled under her chin. People yelled out, asking her if she was all right. She ignored it all. The beautiful makeup she had applied earlier was smeared, and her eyelashes became stuck together with moisture each time she blinked.

The night was darkening more and more, and all Lorraina wanted to do was collapse in a nice warm bed. Instead, she had no idea where she was. As she continued to lose blood from where the bullet had grazed her hip and the gash near her temple, she could feel herself grow weaker by the minute. She neared an alleyway and saw shadows.

"Aye, who's out there?" some man called out to her.

Lorraina said nothing. She could no longer form words. She could barely focus on any of the faces staring back at her as she felt along the brick wall.

"I said, who's out there?" the voice repeated.

"Just shoot me," she said monotonously. "I'm already dead!"

Energy-less, Lorraina slid down the wall and her butt landed on the cool pavement. She exhaled shakily and placed her head against the brick behind her. She could hear rushed footsteps approach her. As she opened her eyes leisurely, she counted four men with big statures overlooking her. They had weird stares. One guy looked lustful, while another looked at her jewelry with excitement. A third guy held a gun to her in panic, and the fourth stood off as though he was the lookout.

"Give me those diamonds!" the guy with the gun ordered.

"Forget the diamonds. What do we have here? You open for business, baby?"

"What's with all the blood? You on your period?"

The conversations went on around her, as Lorraina blinked slowly, and then her head lolled to the side.

"She's gone, bro. Must be high or something."

Lorraina kept her eyes closed involuntarily and could feel movement all around her. She could feel someone yanking at her clothing and her wrists. She could sense that her earrings were being taken out of her ears, and her rings were being slipped off her fingers. She could even feel the men's hands sliding between her thighs and cupping the curve of her buttocks. But her energy was low and her ability to move or defend herself was even lower. She did nothing as the robbers took away her accessories and fondled her body in the process.

"Hey! HEY! Back away from her! Leave her alone!"

The men that were surrounding her stopped what they were doing, seconds before they all took off running, probably in the opposite direction. Lorraina's head pounded, and her heart rate had slowed dramatically. She could no longer open her eyes or make out any sounds. She welcomed peace as she felt the softness of leather wrap around her bare thighs. Then she succumbed to the darkness that surrounded her.

***

Lorraina woke up from what felt like a deep
slumber. She had a crook in her neck, and there
were several thick tubes running in and out of her
body. She also felt numb from the collarbone down
and could see that her clothes were now replaced
with a blue-green hospital gown. As she moved, her
body weight felt magnified. It was like a ton of
bricks were on top of her as she tried to lift her leg.
Miraculously, nothing moved, nor did she feel any
pain.

She briefly wondered where she was and
attempted to move her arm to reach for the cracked
cell phone nestled on her lap.

"Ah, ah…stop moving," came a voice from
across the room.

It was a masculine, strong timbre that was
commanding yet gentle. Lorraina, in all her
numbness and confusion, did not know whom the
voice belonged to, but her heart warmed at the
sound for some reason. "Just relax."

"Where am I?" she questioned. "Who are
you?"

"It's Jhalil, silly." He caressed her cheek.
"What do you remember?"

Perhaps this was a dream. She shrugged and
continued to eye him.

"Nothing."

"You were shot, Rain. I found you
surrounded by guys in an alley," Jhalil explained
carefully. "Do you remember any of that?"

She could not say that she did.

"I don't know. Shot? I got a shot? Where?"

"No, you *were* shot," he continued and stood
up. He walked over to hold her still numb,

trembling fingers. "The bullet hit your hip, and you were hit with a gun to the side of your face. The doctor said that you may not hear clearly for a little while because of the impact, swelling, and bruising, but your eardrum wasn't damaged. So that's a good thing."

"What happened? Why was I shot? Who shot me?" Lorraina questioned. There was a perplexed expression on her face, and she knew that he was probably just as confused as she was. She could not recall anything that had happened prior to waking up even if her life depended on it.

"Kylie."

"Kylie? Who is Kylie? Why did she shoot me?"

Jhalil's brows crinkled as he studied her face. She was completely serious and clueless with every question that tumbled from her oversized and puffy lips. Her mouth was swollen, most likely from the anesthesia.

"Lorraina, don't be silly. Wait a minute. You...you..." he trailed off, and then thought about it. He swallowed hard before speaking, "Do you even remember who I am?"

Reluctantly, she shook her head back and forth.

Jhalil's eyes closed tightly. He began to pray rapidly and wept as the words fell from his tongue. Lorraina watched in silence and attempted to figure out what had transpired to cause her to land in a hospital bed with the odds against her. She grew teary eyed because she had no idea who this handsome man was, but she appreciated him giving her the information she needed. Lorraina closed her eyes and listened to him wrap up his prayer and then kiss her hand.

"Get some rest. We'll figure this thing out later."

She nodded and watched him maneuver around the room until sleep claimed her again.

***

"So, what you're telling me is that I can't remember anything because of the anesthesia that was used?" Lorraina asked and stared at the Hispanic doctor as if he had four heads. Her eyes began to water, her heart tripled in beat, and her patience grew thin as she attempted to understand the foolishness that was coming out of his mouth. "But…but HOW? Why? Why was I the anomaly? How can you reverse this?"

"Shhh. Ma'am, please hear me out," the physician said with panic. "This does not necessarily mean that it is long-term. In fact, short-term memory loss is common after a surgery for one-tenth of patients. Please understand that in most cases the memory returns within a few days, weeks, or even months. Of course, we're definitely hoping that the latter does not occur."

"MONTHS?" Lorraina cried out. "No, there HAS to be something you can do! What am I going to do on my job, or with my family and friends, assuming I have all of that? How am I going to relearn everyday activities? This is insane!"

"I'm afraid all we can do is monitor you from here on out. Until we see improvement, I'm going to schedule a biweekly checkup," he promised and then turned to Jhalil, who looked on in shock. "Is this your family member or spouse? Perhaps he can monitor your sleeping habits and help you in these crucial, very weird stages as you adjust to everything."

Lorraina looked to Jhalil, to the doctor, and then back again. Things had begun to look up for her. Feeling was working its way back into her limbs and she was able to move around more without the help of Jhalil and the nursing assistants. Her day had been capped with the horrible news that she may not ever remember her life before she was induced into a medical coma.

"So that's all you can say? That's all you can give me, as far as an explanation? This is bulls…!"

"Hey!" Jhalil shouted and interrupted her, "I understand you're upset. But the Lorraina I remembered didn't just give up on life. The Lorraina I remembered had turned her life around from what I heard, hated curse words, and anything not pleasing to God. Calm down. God is yet in control and this minor setback is not about to take YOU ten steps back, you hear me? I am here with you, and for you."

"I don't even know you," Lorraina sobbed frantically. "How do I know that I can trust you? I can't remember anything, much less my name! What about my job and my life outside of here? What about my family and friends? I wouldn't be that selfish to ask you to help me out like this."

Jhalil shushed her and gently pulled her face around so that she could look at him. "Once upon a time, I was in love with you and ran away. Once upon a time, you were my best friend in just a short amount of time. Once upon a time, you trusted me more than you trusted yourself. Whether it's a week or a month, let me *help* you until you're better."

Lorraina sat silent for a moment while tears stained her cheeks.

101

"I'm afraid there is more, Ms. McCall," the doctor hesitated. "During surgery, we took a sample of blood and ran a few tests. We found something alarming. Now, you've been through a traumatic experience and in no way do I want to upset you more or discourage you, but…"

"But what?" she repeated.

Jhalil reached out for her trembling hands.

"Ms. McCall, I'm going to have you return to my office in another week so that we can be certain of your diagnosis."

Lorraina shook her head in confusion. "Speak. TALK! What diagnosis?"

"Regretfully, Ms. McCall, I must inform you that we found many abnormal cells in your blood work, and it could potentially be cancer. As I said, we'll have you in again in our office for a more in-depth follow-up. But for now, I need you to get some rest and try to relax."

"Try to relax after being diagnosed with cancer?" Lorraina asked sarcastically and then chuckled. "Yeah, okay. I don't care what you say! I'm not accepting that. I'm not accepting any of that!"

She attempted to stand but forgot about the tubes attached to her body, and the IV drip in her arm. Her foot stumbled clumsily, and if not for Jhalil's quick reaction, she would have taken a tumble. As she inhaled and exhaled deeply, she began to weep uncontrollably and cry out. The sound was heart wrenching and caused Jhalil's own eyes to water.

"Just let me die! I'm going to die anyway!" Lorraina screamed so loudly that her voice became hoarse instantly. "God hates me! Why else would He allow this? Just let me die! I'm already…dead."

The doctor lowered his head and excused himself while Jhalil shushed her and held his face against hers. He rocked their bodies back and forth and cried with her for a little while longer. Lorraina could not believe that this was now her reality. But even with her memory loss, and the news of her possible sickness, she was confident that she could call on her father in heaven. As easy as it was to believe that He had forsaken her, she knew that was not the case.

With Jhalil's help, and her relentless prayers, Lorraina knew that things would be okay. Different, but okay.

Chapter Thirteen

"Who is that?"

Lorraina looked to where Jhalil's index finger was pressed against the image of her and another woman. On her lap was a large photo album that they paged through leisurely. He would ask her who a particular person was, and then once she correctly guessed, he would give her background information on that person. She thought for a second, swallowed hard, and then shook her head in defeat.

"I'm not sure."

"That's the assistant pastor of your church," Jhalil said softly. "You remember who he is?"

He pointed to another man that she was half-hugging. They both wore their civic attire and had bright smiles stretched across their faces. Lorraina squinted in concentration. This memory thing was tearing her apart. She could not remember anything to save her life and it bothered her.

"I—I don't know. I'm sorry."

"You don't need to be sorry. We're taking it one day at a time, remember? This is one of the deacons who visited you in the hospital. His wife is one of your pulpit assistants," Jhalil explained and touched his lips to her forehead. "Don't you dare apologize, you hear me? You're doing well."

Lorraina sighed and paged through a few more photographs. The room was silent as she took it all in. With every image, she looked so content and so *happy*. It was nothing like how she felt now. She was depressed, frustrated, and grumpy much of the time. She could not remember smiling once since she was discharged from the hospital and was forced to begin her "new" life.

She could feel the warm tears welling up in her eyes.

"Hey, hey, please don't cry. You know I hate to see you cry."

Lorraina shrugged and put her hands in the air helplessly. "I can't help it. This is so annoying...and so unfair!"

"At times, life can be unfair. You're right. But don't let it take away that pretty smile and that zeal for life. Before all of this, I remember you being so strong and in control of your life. Don't let this setback define you...it's time to tackle it and CONQUER it."

Lorraina nodded to his encouraging words and wiped her eyes. "I hear you. I just hope God hears my prayers."

"He will. There's a lesson in all of this," Jhalil affirmed. "Even for me. I'm learning and evolving, and my eyes have never been more open."

"What are you learning, if you don't mind me asking? Are you learning how much of a pain taking care of a woman is?" Lorraina asked jokingly.

"Not at all," he said with a smile. "I'm enjoying our time together. I'm glad God allowed me to have this second chance with you."

"Second chance with *me*? Wait. We were together before?"

Jhalil was quiet for a moment. "That's a conversation for another day."

"No, tell me. I want to know. Obviously, I don't remember *anything*. What kind of relationship did we have? Was I good to you?"

"We had a…strange arrangement, I'd say, but you were *so* good to me. We weren't together long, but what we did share was incredible."

"Wow." Lorraina shook her head. "And what else?"

Jhalil licked his lips. "Even though you meant the world to me, I let you down. I hurt you in unimaginable ways and instead of talking to God about it, I ran to an ex-girlfriend for solace and lost you in the process. Since then, I've been in my own personal hell because I didn't trust my instincts."

"You've been in your own personal hell? What do you mean? What happened?"

"I lost the love of my life because I was disobedient and didn't follow God's timing. Instead, I jumped on the first opportunity to satisfy myself. Like a fool, God revealed to me my wife, from the name and right down to the way she looks. Yet, I didn't pay attention, and now I have to deal with the consequences of my sins."

"I'm sorry to hear that. So…who is she? Who's the love of your life that you're speaking of? I don't understand."

"She's you," he said simply.

"*Me?*"

"You," he repeated.

"What are you saying?" Lorraina questioned.

Jhalil smiled knowingly. "It's a lot to take in. Don't worry your pretty little head about it. Let's go back to these flash cards, okay?"

Lorraina was even more perplexed but decided that she would figure out what he was talking about another day. She nodded to his suggestion and looked at the first index card that he held up. "Milwaukee is a city. It's also my birthplace," she answered.

"Good," he said and nodded. He replaced the card with another one.

For thirty minutes each day, they sat across from each other. Jhalil would hold up a flash card, and Lorraina would recite the word and definition. If she needed help, he would give her hints and then quiz her again.

It was so elementary, but so necessary. With each day, Lorraina grew sharper and sharper, and she could tell that her memory was gradually returning. Things that were once a blur to her somehow began to work its way back into her remembrance. She was also grateful for his hard work. Not many men would put their lives on hold to take care of a woman who they once dated.

Their back-and-forth session went on for another few minutes before Lorraina stood up. "Okay, I just need a little break. I'm going to go take a shower and stretch my legs. Is that cool?"

"Oh, yeah, go ahead," he said absently and focused on organizing the flash cards back into their box.

Almost an hour passed before he heard from her again. Jhalil glanced towards the master bedroom when he heard her voice. He was standing at the stove making breakfast food for dinner. Pancake batter was before him, and scrambled eggs with chopped up onion, peppers, and sausage were sizzling on the stove. He should not have left his food unattended, but at that moment, Lorraina's well being was most important.

"Rain?" he called out.

When she didn't answer, he wiped his hands on a dishrag and then made his way into the master bedroom. Cautiously, he peeked his head around the door of the master bathroom where he saw Lorraina wrapped in a terry cloth towel. She was still in the shower, and the water still poured down on her. He could sense that the water was hot even from where he stood, and the steam was thick. All of the mirrors were coated with fog. He could only imagine how warm the droplets felt on her bare skin.

Lorraina had her back to him. Her forehead was pressed to the wall, along with both of her hands. She cried softly and spoke with frustration through her tears.

"Of all things, God, why did You take my memory away from me? Why is the doctor telling me I have cancer?" she cried out. "Why are You ruining my life? Why do You hate me so much?"

Jhalil waited for a moment as she continued to pray and plead to God. He did not want to interrupt, but when her hands balled into fists and began to pound on the wall, he decided to slide the shower door open and step inside with her.

With the water bearing down on him and drenching his clothes, he grabbed her forearms. "Calm down, sweetheart," he whispered over the water. "Shhh. I'm here."

She continued to pound her fists against the wall and then sobbed loudly. "It's not fair! It's not right! Why did God punish me with cancer, Jhalil? I could DIE from this!"

"But you won't!" he affirmed, rubbing her back. "Calm down!"

"What if I never get my memory back? What if my life is never the same?" she panicked, beginning to hyperventilate.

"BREATHE and calm down! Look at me, look at me. You're going to hurt yourself! Calm down."

"I don't care! I'm going to die anyway!"

"Shhh. Stop talking like that," he scolded her. "I know this is all foreign to you and confusing, and overwhelming, but stop speaking that in the atmosphere. You're not going anywhere. Can I share something with you?"

Against his chest, she nodded. Her arms were trembling around him as she hugged his waist.

"I was talking to God the other day, and I was praying. I told Him that I was nervous taking on this responsibility. I was nervous to be the one helping you get back on your feet. I asked Him for strength, and He revealed something very important to me."

She sniffled and looked up at him. "What did He reveal?"

"He said that this situation may not make sense, but He's intentional, and never failing. He allowed you to get to a place where you needed Him and must rely on Him. He took your memory away so that you wouldn't remember the things that you once ran to in times of trouble. Like sex and liquor. Instead, you'll run to Him and have no choice but to trust in Him," Jhalil explained.

She began to speak but he put his finger to her lips.

"He took away all those men who were in your life to use and abuse your body for a reason. You were beginning to idolize what they did for you, and I'll be the first to admit, you were my muse too," Jhalil said. "I had to lose you and put God first in my life again, before He gave me a second chance with you."

109

Lorraina nodded to his words. A single tear rolled down her cheek. She seemed to understand the more he talked.

"He presented the doctors with that cancerous talk so that He could SHOW you that He's still in control, and He's still your healer. Don't you see? He knows exactly what you need. You just have to trust in Him," Jhalil added.

His words seemed to resonate in her spirit as she broke down in tears again. This time, she was not hysterical. She simply raised her hand, and whispered to the ceiling, "Thank You, Jesus."

"Now, He revealed one more thing to me," Jhalil said with a sarcastic look on his face.

Lorraina continued to hug him with one arm. "What?"

"He said that if we don't turn off this shower, my water bill will be high!" Jhalil joked.

Lorraina's laugh, which now sounded refreshed and renewed, echoed throughout the foggy bathroom. Carefully, he stepped out of the warm spray, and helped her out. Without glancing at her body, he helped her remove the soaked towel, and replaced it with a dry one.

"Thank you," she whispered.

"Hmm?"

Jhalil peeled his wet shirt off. As he tugged it over his head and tossed it to the floor, he was surprised to find Lorraina right up under him.

"I said *thank you*," she repeated.

She pressed her body to him. One of her hands cupped the back of his head and then she pulled him down to kiss his unexpected mouth.

For several long moments, their lips collided sensually. It had been so long since he last kissed her, and he instantly remembered how addicted he had become to her once upon a time. She was like a drug; she was a beautiful, tantalizing drug that would not get out of his system no matter how hard he tried.

His hands fell to the curve of her backside and held her in place against him. His mind went back to their sinful nights where she was willing and ready to do anything for him and with him. They would do everything together, at any time and at any place; they would make love, have sloppy, drunk sex, and even publicly fool around. He could not believe this was the same woman. Things had changed so much since then, but all the old memories continued to flood his mind and taint his thoughts.

Even now, he forced himself to break free from her soft lips because there was no telling what his hands would do next. Jhalil wiped his mouth and looked away as he caught his breath. Lorraina simply smiled. Her lips were now swollen from their passionate kiss. She fastened the towel together around her body, turned on the balls of her feet smoothly, and then sauntered out of the bathroom.

He shook his head in thought and distractedly followed the silhouette of her ample buttocks and shapely hips until he could no longer see her. Jhalil glanced down at his lower half and prayed for strength and willpower. A cold shower would suffice.

"Lord, help me fight this temptation," he whispered.

Chapter Fourteen

Lorraina's follow-up appointment rolled around and as anxious as she was, she knew that she had to face the doctors and learn more of her diagnosis. Jhalil's revelations and support gave her peace, strength, and hope to face the appointment with confidence. It also helped that he had taken off work to accompany her. But she could not deny the nerves that were at the pit of her stomach. Still, she was hoping for the best.

The waiting room was cold and filled with other patients. Some were young adults, others were elderly, and then there was Lorraina. She looked completely healthy on the outside. She was dressed casually in her jeans, hooded pink sweater, and matching pink shoes. Her hair was in a sleek, neat bun, and she wore tinted lip gloss.

Although well put together, she could potentially be walking around with cancer cells in her body. It unnerved her. Her leg shook as she waited for her name to be called.

On cue, the receptionist peered over her red, wire-rimmed glasses and called out, "Ms. McCall?"

"Yes." She stood up and followed a young nurse to the back. Jhalil followed closely behind with his hand on her back.

There, another nurse quickly and skillfully took Lorraina's vitals, and gathered blood work and urine samples before patting her shoulder.

"Feel free to get comfortable. There's a gown folded on the bed for you. The doctor will be right with you," the nurse said and applied sanitizer to her hands.

"Thank you," Lorraina spoke softly with a smile.

Jhalil looked away as she quietly changed into the gown and then sat on the bed with her legs swinging off. She extended her foot and nudged him with the tip of her toes that were painted in a bright green color.

"How're you feelin'?" he asked her.

"I'm cool." She shrugged. "Surprisingly very calm."

"Good. That was my prayer for you."

As Jhalil completed his sentence, the door opened behind them and in walked a chipper doctor. He was different from before and was more excited than what Lorraina expected. She was not sure why he was in such a good mood, especially to discuss something as somber as cancer and what life would look like for her.

"Ms. McCall, good to see you. You too, Mr...?" The doctor extended his hand to Jhalil.

"Mr. Harrison."

"And what exactly is your relationship to Ms. McCall?"

"He's my fri—," Lorraina began to say.

"*Boyfriend*," Jhalil interrupted.

"Oh, okay," the doctor spoke slowly, and then smiled away his confusion. "So, it's completely all right with you if we discuss a few things?"

"Yes, of course," Lorraina said with a nod.

"Well, this visit was expected to be long and drawn out, Ms. McCall. But I'd like to get it over and done with, if you don't mind. There is no need to waste your time or mine." He smiled again.

Lorraina swallowed hard and looked at the X-ray that he held up. "What am I looking at? Is it aggressive? What's the black area?" she questioned frantically.

The doctor chuckled.

"Why is this funny to you?" Lorraina snapped and stood up. She could not believe the audacity and the lack of professionalism from this physician. She looked over at Jhalil, who was just as puzzled.

"Please, sit down. It's hilarious to me for one simple reason," the doctor said and handed the X-ray over to her shaky hands. He spoke hurriedly because he saw that she was becoming upset with his upbeat behavior. "Cancer has and never was present in your body, Ms. McCall. What we thought was cancerous blood cells was actually the result of a malfunction on the equipment that we used."

Lorraina's eyes widened. "WHAT? So, you're saying...?"

"Ms. McCall, on behalf of my firm, and the doctor who gave you the original diagnosis, I would like to both congratulate and apologize to you. You are cancer-free, and as healthy as someone your age should be."

The world seemed to stop and Lorraina's heart soared in relief. She asked the doctor to repeat himself before screaming out in joy.

"Oh, my God! It's a miracle!"

"That, it is," the doctor said compassionately. He stood up and extended his arms to her. "I'm ecstatic for you, Ms. McCall. You don't have *anything* to worry about."

"Thank you," she whispered and patted his back a final time. Tears were now coming down her face and once he dismissed himself, she jumped into Jhalil's open arms.

"Didn't I tell you?" he exclaimed with tears brimming his own eyes. "God had the final say! You had nothing to be afraid of!"

All Lorraina could do was thank God over and over as they embraced and cried. She could not have been more grateful. So many people on a day-to-day basis would leave the hospital in tears and with little hope that they would beat cancer or some other fatal ailment and disease. Lorraina was not one of them. She was healed and given a new chance at life, and she vowed never to take it for granted. She also vowed never to question God's plan for her life; after all, His plans were perfect and intentional.

Hand in hand, the two walked out of the cold and solemn hospital and headed back home with the warmth of the sun bearing down on their backs. But it was really the love of the *Son*—God's Son—that truly comforted them. Life was good, and now that Lorraina was feeling and doing much better, Jhalil had other plans in mind.

"Can I take you somewhere?"

Lorraina looked over at him from the passenger seat. Her eyes were still coated with tears of joy and her voice had become raspy from praising God repeatedly. "Somewhere like what?"

"Out of the country. Somewhere beautiful and relaxing," he explained. "Me and a couple of other bishops have a missionary trip in Jerusalem, at the end of the month. I just want you to get away from everything that's been going on."

Lorraina did not say a word for the longest time. She continued to glance out of the window as they rode down the street nearly fifty miles an hour. She was still flying high about the good news, and now he wanted to take her somewhere to celebrate and do only God knows what else.

"I don't know," she admitted. "You've done so much for me already. You don't have to spend a single dime on me anymore."

"That's nonsense. I *want* to do this for you," he said. "So, what do you say? We'll just get away for a few days. Nothing major."

Lorraina thought about it. It was not like she had to report to work. She had broken free from any major responsibilities with her short-term memory loss, and this would be a free trip where she could totally kick her feet up in the sweet company of Jhalil.

Swallowing hard, and looking over at him, she spoke with confidence, "I would love to go with you. But tell me more. You said you and a few bishops? What exactly do you do?"

"I'm a pastor," he said humbly. "One of the youngest members of the Church of God in Christ network. I'm currently obtaining my Master's in Theology and have been under the mentorship of several bishops, so that I can one day govern my own church."

"What? That's amazing. So, is that what you've always done?"

Jhalil chuckled and turned on his right signal. The slow ticks of the signal filled the car. "No, not at all. God called me to this position about four months ago. I was one of the unlikely candidates with my past, my baggage, and all my flaws. Trust me, I never asked for this or saw it coming. It has been crazy—in a *good* way—seeing how much I've grown spiritually in just a short time."

Lorraina nodded, impressed. "Did I know you then?"

Jhalil nodded and bit his lip. "You knew me well. I was a mess but like I said before, God knew when to separate us. He also knew that this season was the right time to bring us back together again. If we had kept going at the rate we were going, who knows where we'd each end up?"

"God, I just wish I remembered all of this," Lorraina sighed.

"Sometimes it's best to let the past go, and to relish in the *now*." Jhalil grabbed her hand and kissed the back of it. "God just wants us to focus on moving forward. Just think about all of the promises He has in store for us? There's no need to look at what's behind us when we know what's ahead."

"That is so true. How are you always so confident? You always know what to say."

"Baby, when I say it's *all* God...I truly mean that."

Lorraina smiled at his nickname for her. They were friends and had gotten so close in just a short time, but she could not deny the fuzzy feeling she got whenever he called her sweet names or kissed the back of her hand. He was so handsome and charming, and she could not suppress the excitement of soon going on vacation with him.

She had not traveled much as far as she could remember, and she certainly had never been to Jerusalem. This was a new life for her, but she was confident that God was leading her to bigger and better things. She planned to make the most of her life and whether her memory returned or not, she was going to love this journey.

***

The month marched on, and it was time to whip out their passports and head to the Holy Land. Lorraina packed nothing but dresses and sandals, while Jhalil's suitcase contained civic attire and a few suit jackets for his church conferences. Their suite was a few miles from the Mount Herzl National Cemetery and was as gorgeous as the brochures that she had seen on the flight over.

After a quick nap, Jhalil was off to do missionary work, while she stayed behind and soaked up the sun. Her melanin was already golden and beautiful, but there was just something about the Holy Land that she fell in love with immediately. It could have been the weather, remarkable sands, and surrounding waters. It could have also been the fact that her Savior had walked these very streets thousands of years ago, ministering, preaching, teaching, and even dying for her sins.

Jhalil returned to their resort after almost three hours and had the biggest smile on his face. "Get dressed. I have a surprise for you."

Lorraina didn't need to be told twice. She dressed in a flowy maxi dress and pinned her hair up. The two ate a quick, catered lunch and then boarded the complimentary shuttle. The tour guide drove them almost two hours away to a river where a crowd of people awaited in white clothing.

"What's going on?" Lorraina asked in confusion. She looked at the faces of all the crying people. Some were praising God and others were praying loudly. There were men and women far and wide who looked sickly, along with a few children. "What is this?"

"This is the Jordan River. We're going to baptize a few people today, including you. I really believe your healing lies in the river. You trust me?"

"I do...but..." Lorraina said hesitantly under her breath. She looked down at her clothes and felt inappropriately dressed. Before she could even speak, he put his hand over hers and kissed it.

"I have something for you to put on in place of your clothes. Come on. Just trust me."

Through the sea of bodies, Jhalil and Lorraina made their way to the front, and she was given a white garment to wrap around her frame. One of the female assistants helped her pull her dress from beneath the linen frock and cover her hair with a swim cap. Lorraina was relieved that she had thought ahead and pinned her hair for the day. Then, one of the pastors who had flown on their same flight, suddenly appeared before her and extended his hand.

"Are you ready, Sister Lorraina?"

She had no choice but to be, as she nodded and took his hand. With the help of Jhalil, she stepped into the cool water. Instantly, she felt like Jesus Himself was embracing her. She felt a weight lift from her body, and tears sprang to her eyes involuntarily.

Around her, a choir of six sang Israel Houghton's "Moving Forward," and people worshipped and prayed. Jhalil stood behind her, while the pastor poured blessed oil on his hand. He formed a cross on her forehead with his index finger, prayed over her, and then recited a few scriptures.

"We're now going to baptize this young lady. Saints, while we do so, please pray and cover her as she steps into a *new* life," the pastor announced. He nodded to the surrounding clergy, so that everyone was prepared.

Lorraina folded her arms across her chest, closed her eyes, and felt her body become completely submerged in the healing waters. As she surfaced from the water, seconds later, all she could see was the green of the leaves on the trees, the rich brown hue of the sands and mountains in the distance, and the blue skies above. Her senses were better than ever, and she could smell the freshness of the air around her. Jhalil helped her stand completely, while one of the female ministers wiped her down and then wrapped her in a dry towel.

Without thought, Lorraina began to speak in tongues. Like a movie trailer, her life flashed before her eyes and everything that she had once forgotten about came back to her remembrance. Lorraina's childhood, adolescence, and the positive moments in her adulthood resonated in her spirit. It was a miracle. Her memory was back, and she could do nothing but raise her hands and cry out in gratitude.

Jhalil had been right. To the side of her, she could hear him thanking God as well. This visit to the Jordan River was just what was needed, and she was restored. Her eyes seemed clearer, her heart was now purer, and the tears would not stop flowing.

"Thank You, God! Thank You for restoration," she cried out.

While she continued to dry off and sing her praises, the crowd grew more and more scarce as more people were baptized. Lorraina stayed by Jhalil's side until everyone was tended to. The Spirit of God was stronger than ever and there was nothing but joyous tears being shed. It was a sight to behold, and one that she would remember for the remainder of her life.

Finally, when darkness blanketed the sky and night came, the shuttle arrived to take them back to their suite.

Jhalil rubbed the back of her head and then massaged her neck briefly. "How are you feeling?"

"I...I can't even express how I feel right now. There was nothing like it," she attempted to explain. "Thank you for bringing me here."

"Thank you for trusting me and coming along with me," he said and then summoned her over with a finger. "Come here."

She followed him over to where he sat and kissed him.

Chapter Fifteen

When they returned to the States, Lorraina could not deny the fire that had been reignited in her soul. She wrote letters to everyone that she hurt while living in sin, including her old church members, and the men she had slept with carelessly. Deacon Donnell had lost his rights and privileges within the church but was remorseful for his actions as well. Still, Lorraina could only blame herself. She apologized for being weak and for playing with so many others' hearts and lives. She visited her grandmother's gravesite to thank her for raising her well and took each day at a time. The trip to the Holy Land had restored her mind, body, and soul, and she was looking forward to the next step.

Currently, they sat next to each other in preparation for a business meeting that Jhalil had initiated. He was just weeks away from opening his own church and was working out the kinks. He wanted everything to be perfect and had called his mentor to send over a few pastors who could help. They waited now for one more person to show. Only then would the meeting start.

Lorraina would be his Executive Administrative Assistant for the time being and was looking forward to seeing him preach every Sunday and Tuesday. He was a great speaker, and she knew that he would inspire a multitude of young men especially.

"So, there's no first lady in your life, huh?" one of the elders joked and nudged Jhalil.

Lorraina looked up from the notes she was taking. Jhalil looked over at her and smirked. Her cheeks warmed with a blush as he said his next words.

"I'm working on it."

At that moment, the door opened to the side of them and in walked a man with broad shoulders and he had the stature of somebody's bodyguard or a football player. He towered over everyone and his presence commanded respect and attention. He extended his hand to a few of the people closest to him and then turned to Lorraina and Jhalil. As he removed his dark sunglasses, Lorraina's breath caught in her throat.

"Hello, nice to meet you. I'm Curtis."

Jhalil shook the man's hand and then placed his hand on the small of Lorraina's back. When she did not right away speak to the pastor, Jhalil looked over and spoke up.

"Curtis, this is my lady, Lorraina." Jhalil pushed her forward so that she stood in front of him. He placed a hand on her shoulder. "I'm not sure why she's acting so shy though."

Lorraina reluctantly extended her hand but found it hard to speak. Standing before her was a man from her past, and somebody who she never imagined running into again.

"Hello, beautiful. It's good to meet you."

"Hi," Lorraina said simply and forced a smile. "Good to meet you too, Curtis."

"Call me Curt, beautiful."

"I'll call you Curtis, and I would appreciate it if you didn't call me anything other than my name," she said with a brewing attitude and then walked away.

Jhalil looked puzzled while Curt simply smiled. His eyes followed her around the room where she returned to her original seat at the conference table and kept her head low. Jhalil began to speak up and apologize on her behalf, but Curt held his hand up.

"No need to explain. That's a woman for ya. Mood swings and eye rolls," he chuckled. "I'm used to it."

Jhalil clapped his hands twice and got everybody's attention. "All right, ladies and gentlemen, we're ready to start."

As everyone filed to their seats, Jhalil took his stance up at the front of the room. He had a presentation that he had prepared for everyone. Lorraina turned off the lights and settled back in her seat. By then, Curt had moved to sit directly beside her. She could feel that his eyes were on her as she turned to Jhalil.

Midway through the presentation, she felt Curt's hand land on her thigh under the table.

"Would you stop?" she whispered.

"Funny because you once told me *'don't stop,'*" he retorted.

Lorraina looked around at the other people in the room. No one seemed to pay attention to them, but she felt like they were speaking at a high volume. Her cheeks were flushed, and her heart thumped at a speed that did not seem healthy. It echoed in her eardrum.

Curt's stare stayed with her for the remainder of the meeting and even when things ended, he boldly touched her shoulder and leaned so close that she could feel his lips against her collarbone. She pulled away from him roughly and wiped the area of her neck that he had touched.

"So, are you two dating?" he asked. "I sure hope not. That would make things rather interesting around here."

"That's none of your business," she snapped as quietly as she could, "and get your hands off of me!"

Still, even with raising her voice, no one seemed to notice their exchange. Jhalil, who was laughing with another woman at the front of the room, never once turned and saw Lorraina's look of distress.

"Whoa, whoa," he spoke cautiously. "Is everything okay? What did I do?"

"Curt, stop acting like this. You're making me uncomfortable, and you're going to make yourself look stupid if Jhalil finds out what happened between us."

"Ah, but you aren't that stupid to tell him. I mean, I know your man would hate to find out how the very table we're seated at, is the same color and shape of the one that I held your legs down on, and ate your…"

"STOP IT!" All eyes focused on them and Lorraina felt embarrassed for her outburst. At the same time, she wanted Jhalil to look up and rescue her from this disrespectful man. He knew what he was doing.

"I was just going to say ate your peach cobbler. What?" he spoke sarcastically and evilly. Then his demeanor and tone changed as he turned to Jhalil. "Hey, man, I'm going to call it a night. Thanks for inviting me out. We'll definitely be in touch."

"Cool, man. Thanks again," Jhalil said with a smile, but his eyes were on Lorraina in shock.

The second they left the conference room, she knew he had 101 questions.

"What was that about?" Those words were the first thing to hit Lorraina's ears when she closed the car door. Jhalil looked over at her. He was clearly baffled by her behavior. "Rain, you hear me talking to you. Why did you treat Pastor Curtis that way?"

"He's a PASTOR?" she questioned. "And treat him like what? I spoke to him and gave my input when he asked questions. What are you talking about?"

"You know *exactly* what I'm talking about. Don't act like that. You were noticeably different the minute he walked in. What's wrong?"

"Nothing's wrong. I just...I don't have a good feeling about him. Do we have to work with *him*?" Lorraina asked.

She would not dare tell Jhalil why she was so disgusted by Curt and the history they shared. After all, it was not a good look to say that she had slept with both men and would ultimately have to work with both men—in ministry, at that. If the congregants ever found out, that was a disaster waiting to happen and she vowed never to stir up a church the way that she had before. She certainly hated to put Jhalil in such a situation.

"He's a good dude. I've hung out with him on a couple of occasions, and I promise, there's nothing to be cautious about."

If only you knew, she thought.

"Besides, he's just coming for a short time to help me get things up and running. It won't be a permanent thing."

"I hope so."

"It's probably just his beard that's making you feel that way," he added jokingly.

Lorraina threw her head forward in a fit of laughter. Jhalil joined in too, and just like that, all was forgotten.

Chapter Sixteen

Despite Jhalil's promises, Curt quickly became a permanent fixture around the budding church, their shared home, and in their lives. Everywhere that Lorraina was, somehow Curt was always in the picture. It unnerved her. She could be doing something as simple as adding a fresh floral arrangement to the women's bathroom, and Curt would pop his head in and ask her if she needed help. He would even show up to their house and claim that he had gotten a message that there would be a prayer meeting there.

None of his advances were working, and she knew what kind of game he was playing. Yet she never told a soul. Although she was not scared, she feared for what Jhalil would do and think if he ever found out.

Just when she thought she let the sins of her past go, Curt had shown up like he was God's gift to the world. He was a constant reminder to her that to every wrongdoing came a consequence. This was the bed that she made, and she was forced to lie in it. This secret was surely an attack from the enemy, and it was going to kill her if she allowed it.

"What should I do…tell him?" she spoke into the phone in a hushed tone. Jhalil was in the room next to her and had good hearing on any good day. She was taking a gamble by even discussing such a topic, but the stress had become too much for her to handle. She had to vent and tell *someone*.

Khloey was on the other line, taking it all in. "No, absolutely not! If you say something, you could lose Jhalil. You know how guys are—big egos and bigger tantrums to match."

"I know, but…what if Curt's dangerous? What if he's some crazy person who can't handle rejection? He's one of the guys I wrote a letter to explaining that I was sorry for playing with their hearts and how I didn't want them to contact me. I think that upset him and he's been in our lives ever since. Jhalil thinks he's a pastor, but I highly doubt that."

"If *you* feel it's safe enough, I would just have a heart to heart with Curt. Do *not* go in person though. I would call him on a public phone—that way he doesn't have your number. If he can't understand it, then you get a restraining order on that fool. At a certain point though, definitely let Jhalil know that he's from your past."

"I guess, but he's been in our home," Lorraina said with a sigh. "There's really no point of secrecy because he knows where I lay my head every night."

A part of her just wanted to hide from the world and the other part of her had the confidence to call Curt now and give him a piece of her mind. But she did neither. Instead, she hung up from her friend and then walked over into the next room.

It was dimly lit, other than the images that flashed around the room from the TV. Jhalil was comfortable in a pair of basketball shorts, long tube socks, and nothing more. Although they were living on a straight and narrow path and had not slept together since reuniting, it was moments like these, when Lorraina had to swallow hard. He was just too fine for his own good. Jhalil had one leg thrown over the back of the couch and the other was planted on the floor.

The man was literally spread-eagled.

He had fallen asleep with a video game controller in his hand and an empty can of soda was nestled near his head on the pillow. She grinned and walked over to rid his hands of the equipment. He stretched in his sleep at that moment and knocked her hand down so that it was planted on his lap. Jhalil never stirred awake, but Lorraina now found herself in an uncompromising position. Her face was just inches from his, and her arm was weighed down by his. She could literally feel every inch of him against her.

"Baby," she called softly.

Jhalil continued to snore peacefully.

"Jhalil," she said a little louder. "Wake up."

He never moved. She struggled for a moment to stand up again, and then finally, she had to kiss along his neck to get him to maneuver around. "Mmm, you trying to get something started?" he asked sleepily.

"No, I'm trying to get the feeling back in my arm," she joked. "*Mooooove*, bae."

His eyes took in her position and then he moved around so that she could lie comfortably in his embrace. Her back became flush against his chest, and he rested his chin in her hair. "That better?" he asked.

"Much better."

"Mm, you smell so good," he added as he played in her hair.

She was wearing a pair of stretchy shorts, a lacy camisole that hugged her breasts a little too tightly, and slip-on house shoes. He rubbed a hand over her stomach and knew that she was ticklish there.

"Stop it."

"Or what?" he teased.

Jhalil licked his lips and then pulled her chin towards him so that he could kiss her. She turned around fully in his arms so that their chests were pressed together. Her lips opened and welcomed his tongue as they kissed passionately. Against her body, Jhalil's hands seemed to have a mind of their own, and he could not stop caressing her warm melanin.

She, too, was in a zone. The sexual tension was at an all-time high and she doubted that she would stop his advances. Lorraina boldly straddled his waist and pulled her camisole off. Jhalil took that as his opportunity to kiss along her neck, the tops of her breasts, down her stomach, and then back up to her lips again.

"Tell me what you want," he said aggressively. His breaths were erratic with excitement and anticipation.

"It's wrong…and it's not pure," she admitted. "Moving in together was not the best idea, because I find myself tempted by you."

"In what way?"

"Jhalil, don't do this."

"Just tell me," he begged. "Tell me what you want."

"I want you to make love to me…all night…" she confessed shyly.

"Your wish is my command," he growled.

They kissed again and moved around on the couch until she was below him. Lorraina squirmed in anticipation and wrapped her legs around his waist. Their bodies grinded sensually against each other and made a rhythm that was slow and unlike any other. When his hands settled at her buttocks and began to tug at the elastic of her shorts, she seemed to snap back into reality and gasped.

Lorraina pulled away to prevent any further temptation. Her chest heaved up and down breathily.

Jhalil shook his head and then covered his lap with a pillow. He punched the back of the couch and looked frustrated.

"What's wrong?" she asked.

"You are so sexy."

"And that's a problem?" she laughed as a blush warmed her cheeks.

"That's a *big* problem. I made a vow to God, you, and myself that I wouldn't allow us to go down any of those roads again. Yet here we are…whew." He struggled to catch his breath.

"I hear you." Lorraina wiped her lips and then looked away from his disappointed face. "I'm sorry."

"No, no. Stop apologizing. I just hate that things aren't exactly lined up. Otherwise, well, you'd be pregnant right now."

Jhalil stood up and walked into the kitchen. He headed to the stainless steel refrigerator where he grabbed a bottle of water. Lorraina followed behind him with a laugh and knew that while he was joking, he was also serious. She thought about it for a second and just knew she had to be crazy for her next words. Hesitantly, she rubbed her arm and then leaned against the waist-high countertop.

"You said that things aren't exactly lined up. What do you mean by that?"

"I mean, you know. We're trying to do the right thing and be celibate. We're not married. I just wish things were different in that aspect. I refuse to let you fall short of the glory of God over me, and I know you feel the same."

"I do feel the same, but we're adults, Jhalil. Why can't things be different?"

"We aren't exactly in the position to take that next step. I mean, are we? Are you ready?"

They stared each other down and Lorraina felt her heart soar. She threw his words back at him, "Just tell me what you want, baby."

Jhalil held his hand over his heart. "I mean, it's no secret that I want to marry you."

"Mmhmm, and?"

He smiled. "And I want to grow old with you, and with every day fall more in love with you. You know how I feel about you."

"Don't get me wrong, you've helped me get through THE toughest times in my life, and I love where we're headed. But it's so soon. What will people think?" She winked, her words playful. "You know they're going to question us."

He shrugged. "Who cares what they think? People fall in love all the time *literally* at first sight. It's not their lives or journey, it's ours."

Lorraina's heart thumped erratically. She felt beautiful under his gaze as he professed his love and feelings to her. In his eyes, she could see the tears welling up, and she could feel the tears springing to the forefront of her own eyes.

"I need, want, and love you too, Jhalil Harrison," Lorraina purred and wiped at her eyes. "You're so good to me."

"So, what are we waiting for? I know it's informal, but baby, we have nothing to lose. God has allowed us to go through so much together in so little time, and I can promise you, I'm not going anywhere else."

"I'm not going anywhere either!" she vowed and jumped into his arms.

Against her hair, he whispered, "Marry me, baby? Be my wife. Let's conquer life together, and you'll never want for anything."

Lorraina nodded with her head still nestled in the crook of Jhalil's neck. "Yes! I will marry you!" she cried into his shoulder for a moment and then kissed his cheek. "What did I do to deserve you?"

"No, *I'm* the blessed one. I love you, Lorraina," he said before kissing her lips. Their private celebration ended abruptly when the doorbell rang. Lorraina looked over towards the door and then glanced up at Jhalil. "Are you expecting somebody?"

"No." He frowned and walked over to the door. The blinds were closed so he peered through the peephole. "It's Curt," he mouthed.

Lorraina rolled her eyes and shook her head. "Don't let him in," she mouthed back. She ran towards the bedroom to put on a robe, and then peeked out at where Jhalil stood. He seemed to be debating if he should open the door or not.

"Don't let him in," she whisper-yelled.

He walked over to her and then pulled her by the hand into their room. "Why not? What if it's an emergency?"

"Jhalil, it's late. He has your number, right?"

"Yeah."

"Okay, then he can call. We're both undressed, and ready for bed. Whatever he has to tell you can wait until tomorrow. I'm not playing, bae. Don't open that door."

"All right, all right. I hear you. I'll let it go," Jhalil said.

They stayed in the room until they could no longer hear the doorbell ringing. He knocked one final time roughly, and then a few minutes later, the sounds of tires skidding could be heard. Lorraina tiptoed back into the living room and then peeked out of the blinds. She saw no car in sight, nor the silhouette of Curt's husky body.

Only then did she breathe a sigh of relief.

As she turned on her heels, she walked towards the bedroom and heard a loud bang outside. A scream ripped from her lips and caused her to jump so violently that she could swear urine had made its way down her legs. Jhalil ordered her to get back into their bedroom while he investigated what was going on outside.

He shrugged on a T-shirt and then peeked out of the blinds. Nothing but darkness and the shadows of the swaying trees greeted him. "I can't see anything. Grab my gun out of the safe," he added.

Lorraina rushed back inside of their bedroom to open the safe that was conveniently already opened. She fumbled to grab the handgun that had a little weight to it, and she grabbed the box of bullets that were to the right of it.

"Here, baby!" She ran out and to her surprise, Jhalil was greeting Curt as he walked through their doors.

Chapter Seventeen

Quickly, Lorraina hid the gun in the back of her shorts and wrapped her robe a little tighter. She could have smacked Jhalil for opening the door for this creep. Everyone's eyes landed on her as she entered the room fully.

"Oh, hi. I didn't realize we had company."

"Baby, his car broke down up the street and he needed to call for help. Where's your phone?"

"You don't have a phone either?" she asked Curt. "Who leaves the house without their phone?"

He shook his head and raised his hands. "I'm sorry for disturbing your evening. My battery died on my phone, so that's why I decided to walk up this way. I remembered you lived here."

"Oh, you've been here before? Baby, he's been here before?"

Lorraina swallowed and watched Curt like a hawk. He was smiling mischievously, and his eyes were so evil. She knew hate was a strong word, but she could not help but feeling that for him in this moment.

"Yeah, I came because I thought we were having a prayer meeting a few weeks back, but it was at Sister Earline's home," Curt explained. "I thought you knew? The wifey didn't tell you?"

The room grew warm suddenly. Lorraina shifted uncomfortably and she knew that she would have some serious explaining to do later tonight. Jhalil shook his head and seemed to disregard the misunderstanding.

"Nah, I didn't know."

"Yeah, there's a lot you don't know, my man."

"Meaning *what?*" Jhalil wanted to know with a raised eyebrow. He looked Curt up and down skeptically and then glanced back at Lorraina, who was visibly upset. She twirled her fingers nervously and her eyes had suddenly chosen to focus on anything but Jhalil's eyes.

Curt began to speak smugly, "Like the fact that I'd already met your…"

Lorraina interrupted him and extended her hand. Her voice had gotten much softer as her nerves took over. "Hey, grab a seat. Is it raining outside? Your coat is wet. Let me take that."

Curt smiled and seemed to like the fact that he had her right where he needed her. "I didn't want to stay long. I just needed to use a phone, that's all. I'll wait in my car for the tow truck."

Jhalil pulled out one of the stools at the island counter. "That's nonsense, man. You've been helping me so much getting this ministry off the ground. The least I could do is allow you to sit and wait inside. You want anything to drink? Eat?"

Curt sat down and thought about it. He stared at Lorraina, back over to Jhalil, and then back up at her again. "You have any peach cobbler?"

Lorraina began to choke on nothing while Jhalil found it funny. "Did you smell it? She made some for dessert actually."

"Yeah, I love peaches. Love to eat 'em…suck 'em…just devour 'em," Curt retorted with a laugh. "That and water would be great right now. You know, if it's not too much to ask."

"No, it's cool. Baby, grab my phone from the room. I'll get Curt situated in here," Jhalil volunteered.

Lorraina hated that he was so oblivious to Curt's condescending words, stalker-like gazes, and disrespectful undertones. It shook her to the core as she turned and walked as modestly as she could to the back. She prayed that her hips didn't sway as they normally did, nor did her buttocks jiggle as it usually would. There was a monster watching her like a hawk and she could feel him.

Sure enough, as she rounded the corner and turned back around, she saw Curt's eyes on her backside. He stared at her hungrily, as if he could not get enough of her. The way he looked at her, she was reminded of when they first met and the way he had attacked her body sexually. She even caught the wink that he gave her as Jhalil turned to prepare a plate for him. She felt disrespected and violated. It hurt her even more that Jhalil had no clue about what was happening before his eyes.

Lorraina retrieved the cell phone on the bed that Jhalil had carelessly tossed hours before. He had all kinds of missed calls, texts, and a few voice messages. They all came from Curt. She cringed and then gave the phone to Jhalil.

"Baby, I'm going to go lay down. Have a good night, Curt." She waved a hand and walked out.

"Sweet dreams, beautiful."

Her skin crawled each time he called her that. She could cry, but she knew that all she had right now was prayer and faith. Jhalil would be with Curt for God only knows how long, and she feared that Curt would sing like a canary. It was obvious that he still wanted her and had become upset with her, even downright vengeful. After their initial sex adventure, she had blocked his text messages and phone calls; it had probably pissed him off. To add to the letter that she had recently sent out, the man was likely going crazy.

Still, Lorraina closed her door, and knelt on her knees. She began to pray that Curt would find it in his heart to forgive her. She prayed for the strength to be able to tell Jhalil about this monster of a man that sat just feet from her in the kitchen. She even prayed that no more of her mistakes and past sins came back to haunt her.

This was becoming too much.

"Baby?" Jhalil's head was poking in the door, and he looked concerned. Then he seemed to understand what was going on and put his hand over his mouth. "Oh! My bad. Are you praying in here?"

"I was, yes. What's up?" She stood up from her position and sat on the edge of the bed. "Is he still in there?"

"No, he called his roadside assistance company, and said he'd wait in the car. But he did leave you something."

"Oh, okay," Lorraina let out a huff. "That's all he said?"

"Yeah." Jhalil handed her a box. "Was he supposed to say anything else?"

Lorraina shrugged and then offered a smile. She put the gift down on the bed and slapped her palms against her thighs. "No, I was just wondering. I'm glad he got everything figured out."

"Aren't you going to open it up?"

Lorraina looked at the neatly wrapped box. It was eye-catching and although she was curious about its contents, there was no telling what was in the box. She refused to open it up before him and instead, she shook her head and stood up. "Maybe later. Right now, I'm going to clean up the kitchen and then take my shower."

On her way past him, he kissed the side of her face lovingly.

"I'll be back shortly," she promised.

Jhalil watched her toss the robe from around her body and disappear in the bathroom. Lorraina knew that nothing had been said between Jhalil and Curt because his demeanor had not changed. She was confident that she could have a talk with him first to soften the blow. She had to keep reminding herself that just as sure as she had a past, Jhalil had one too. If he loved her as he said, he would be willing to work around the situation. For the fourth or fifth time in the last hour, she said a prayer and then stepped from the relaxing shower.

Leisurely, she dried her body, moisturized her skin with lotion, and then brushed her hair into a neat ponytail.

"Baby?" Her voice echoed off the foggy bathroom walls. All was quiet on the opposite side of the door, so she called out for her fiancé again.

Fiancé.

It was crazy to think that he had proposed, no matter how informal it was. The truth was, she was ready to be his wife—her heart was ready to love unconditionally.

"Jhalil?" she called a final time and then rounded the corner of the master bedroom.

He was seated on the edge of the bed, where she was sitting previously. On his lap was the opened gift that Curt had left for her. To Lorraina's surprise, Jhalil had opened the box and was staring at its contents with one of the coldest expressions she had ever seen grace his handsome face. There was a note in his hand that he had crumbled up slightly, most likely out of anger.

All of the peace that had blanketed her spirit disappeared immediately. She could not read his expression and it scared her to death. She clutched the towel around her body so tightly that her knuckles turned white. "Jhalil, what happened? What's that? What does it say?"

For the longest time, he never looked up or said a word. Finally, as she inched closer to him, he put his hand up. "Don't come any closer to me."

"What are you talking about, baby?"

"Don't 'baby' me!" he yelled.

"Jhalil, I'm trying to understand what's going on. Stop yelling and talk to me," she pleaded in desperation, but he did not seem affected by her forming tears.

Through gritted teeth, Jhalil held up a pair of underwear. It was a size five and resembled every other pair that she wore currently. They were lace and were the same pair that she wore the day she met Curt and had sex with him in her old church office.

In an instant, her world came crashing down. Her body followed suit as she heard the dreaded question, "Lorraina, why does a member of my staff have your *PANTIES*?"

Lorraina stared at her undergarments dangling from Jhalil's hands in horror. The longer she stared, the more she hoped the crimson red panties would disappear. But they never left Jhalil's hand, much in the same way Jhalil's hand never faltered. He was shaking in anger and what she assumed was disappointment. Just like that, her biggest fears were coming true and there was nothing that she could do. There was nothing that she could really say that would make things better. All she had was her side and her truth.

He threw the paper in her direction. Before it could spiral down to the floor, she caught it between her grasp. "Jhalil…"

"READ IT!"

"Baby, before you say anything…"

"Read the letter, Lorraina!" Jhalil had never raised his voice at her this way. Her shoulders jerked in surprise and then she reluctantly looked down to view the crumbled piece of paper. It looked like it had been ripped from a composition notebook and then folded. She could even catch a whiff of cologne—Curt's cologne. She grew sick to her stomach at the thought that he had gone out of his way to ruin her relationship.

Shakily, Lorraina began to read, "'*Roses are red, violets are blue. The secret is out, I had her before you.*' Ugh!"

Jhalil stood up abruptly. He threw the box and her underwear onto the floor and brushed past her. "Rain, I swear to God, you better give me a good explanation otherwise you'll be back on the streets just as soon as I pack your bags. Don't play with me! What is THIS?"

"Calm *down*!"

"I'm not calming down. Remember, this is my house!" He moved swiftly to the closet where most of her things were hanging. He began to discard a few articles of clothing while she attempted to stop him. He shrugged off her hold. "What else don't I know about you? Huh? Let me guess, you slept with him?"

"Y—yes, but it's not like that, baby. I slept with him literally *right* after we met. After we grew close, I broke things off with him, Capri, and whoever else. You know that."

"I didn't know that. It's like you chose to withhold certain information and that's not cool. I've been honest with you from the beginning. When did you sleep with him?"

"I already told you. It was," she thought back quietly and rubbed her arm, "a few days after we met. I swear!"

He shook his head and chuckled painfully. There were tears in his eyes when he whipped around and continued his 21 questions.

"Figures. How many times did he make love to you? Where did he touch you?" he yelled and punched the wall a few times. "God, Lorraina! Why couldn't you have said something in the beginning? Now, you've got me out here looking like a fool, while he smiles in my face. What kind of game are you playing?"

"I'm not playing any game! This is the *very* reason why I didn't want to tell you," she explained. "I didn't want to turn you off then, but I see it really didn't matter. Please hear me out. You know I wouldn't intentionally hurt you."

"Do I? I'm starting to believe I don't know you at all," he retorted coldly. He continued to pull her garments from the shelves and racks and tossed them into one of his duffel bags. "I mean, seriously. Who haven't you slept with?"

His words cut her like a knife, and she immediately grew hot with anger and humiliation. She looked at him incredulously. She was half pissed off by his remarks, and half hurt, especially since there was a hint of sarcasm and disrespect in his tone. Without fully thinking her actions through, Lorraina drew her arm back and with blinding

142

anger, she slapped Jhalil. His head rocked to the side, and she could see the muscles tightening in his neck and around his jawline.

"You knew I had issues! You KNEW why I went to rehab. I was addicted to sex, but I got the help I needed. Don't try to play me."

Jhalil stepped into her face.

Lorraina held her ground and kept her head high. She pointed her finger in his face with every word. "Don't try to shame me because you're hurt right now! You were a ladies' man yourself. Let's not forget who followed whom, outside of the restaurant, the night we met."

"It's neither here nor there, Rain," Jhalil said. He looked frustrated. "I just don't understand. After all the opportunities I gave you, you chose not to tell me about something like this."

"Let it GO, Jhalil! My goodness. What do you want me to say? I'm sorry, okay? I'm sorry for sleeping with Curt! I'm sorry for not telling you! I'm sorry for hitting you. I'm sorry for it all, but don't crucify me," she sobbed. "Don't act like you're perfect and don't have a past. You think I wanted this to come out? You think I expected Curt to come back into my life and stir things up? The man is crazy! Why do you think I was pressing the issue so much not to work with him?"

Jhalil thought about it for a moment. He knew she was right and reluctantly, he agreed. He pressed his forehead to the wall to calm down a bit. Lorraina could see that his shoulders shook and that soft cries were leaving his mouth. Then he turned around to face her finally. His blemish-free skin was stained with tears. The moisture puddled over from his eyes like a never-ending river.

"It's my turn to say I'm sorry. I didn't listen to you, and I overreacted, and that wasn't cool." His voice was shaky with emotions. She could honestly say that she had never seen him look so remorseful or vulnerable. "But let this be a lesson. You have no reason to be afraid to tell me anything whether it happened ten minutes ago, or ten years ago. If we're going to do this, we *must* be honest with each other. You hear me?"

"I hear you," she agreed and nodded. "Like I said, I just didn't know how you'd react but…"

He put his finger to her lips to cut her words off. "Shhh. That's all in the past now. Tomorrow, I'm going to have a heart to heart with him and just let him know that I appreciate all the help he's given to the ministry, but we can't work together. I'm not even going to mention what you two had."

Lorraina smiled weakly and then wrapped her arms around his neck. She rubbed her nose against the side of his face and inhaled his scent. They seemed to breathe each other's air for a moment and then she exhaled completely.

"Can we just start over…for the *third* time?" her words were playful but serious as well.

"C'mere," Jhalil whispered. "We're going to make this right. It may take some healing, some uprooting, and some replanting, but I'm not going anywhere, and I pray you don't either. We've been through way too much to give up now."

"Only God Himself can remove me," she promised, while looking him in the eyes.

Like magnets, their lips collided and stayed connected for a long moment.

Chapter Eighteen

"Baby, wake up."

"Hmm?" Lorraina stirred awake from her deep slumber and glanced up. Jhalil was hovered over her as he whispered. The room smelled of cologne as he moved around and continued to get ready for the day. She assumed he was heading either to a corporate breakfast, or to a church meeting, by the way he was dressed.

"I'm headed out. I should be no more than an hour or so. I'll call you on my way home," he said and kissed her forehead.

"Okay. See you, baby." Lorraina smiled and watched him walk out.

He winked and then closed the door behind him. He was handsome as ever and outfitted in a black shirt and black slacks. A dark grey and black pinstriped suit jacket was draped over his forearm. He accessorized with black diamonds across his wrist and a black matte tungsten pinky ring.

All night, he had tossed and turned. Each time that she asked him if he was okay, he would simply say that he was "thinking." She knew their discussion yesterday probably was weighing heavily on his mind, but he would never admit it. Lorraina hated that she had brought the added stress to his life, but it was better to get things out now than later.

His scent lingered even after an hour later, when she text him about his whereabouts. She started on breakfast and was whipping up the batter to pancakes when she received a text. It was Jhalil telling her he would be another 15 minutes or so. She poured the thick, buttery batter into the sizzling pan with a grin.

"Thank You, God. Things could have gone left, but they didn't," Lorraina said into the atmosphere.

She prepared each plate, neatly folded the napkins, and placed silverware next to each plate. She took a quick, relaxing shower, and then waited for him with two glasses of pulp-free orange juice. She tried not to watch the clock too much.

Meanwhile, across town...

"Hi, can I start you fellas off with anything to drink?"

Jhalil looked up from the menu and knew that only water was his idea of a breakfast, at least until he made it back to Lorraina. His mind was focused on bigger, more important things. Although a prayer breakfast was going on currently, he could not help but to stare down the obnoxiously smug negro directly across from him.

Of course, as fate always had it, he was in the room with Curt at possibly the *worst* time in history. After all, Jhalil's blood was already still seething from what Lorraina had revealed to him. He knew that he was not ready to address the issue with Curt personally, but seeing him now, made Jhalil rethink the situation.

The more he sat across from him, the more he thought of how he touched Lorraina. Jhalil hated that his hands had stroked, caressed, and massaged his woman once upon a time. Jhalil grew angrier and angrier at the fact that someone else's lips had skimmed over Lorraina's. It was sickening.

"Uh, Pastor Jhalil?" one of the ministers cleared his throat and asked cautiously. "You okay over there? Did you want anything to eat?"

146

He rolled his neck around and stretched his back. Then he sat up straighter in his seat and shook his head. He took his eyes off Curt and then rubbed his forehead. "No, I'm good. Can we, uh, wrap this up? I have to speak with Brother Curt in private, please."

"But Pastor, we just got here not long ago…"

"What did I say?" Jhalil snapped and then calmed down some. He noticed the look on everybody's faces while he cleared his throat and then stood up. "Excuse me while I run to the little boy's room."

Silence followed him as he entered the restroom not far away. Jhalil sighed and leaned against the wall. He did not really have to pee, but he did need to keep it cool until he could figure everything out. Perhaps today wouldn't be the best time to give Curt a piece of his mind.

Jhalil checked his phone as it buzzed. It was Lorraina texting him again. She sent a picture of herself making pouty lips at him as if to say she was lonely. Then, not even a second later, she sent another text.

Missing you…come home soon! Food's getting cold.

Even miles away, she knew just what he needed. Jhalil smirked and found peace in the fact that she was craving his presence. He decided to just leave, whether the men were done with their meeting or not. As he turned to exit the restroom, the door opened, and Curt entered.

Jhalil faked a grin and nodded. "Have a good day."

"You good, Pastor? You've been so short with me today."

Jhalil closed his eyes and exhaled. He did not care if it came off as rude. He was exactly four steps away from the door and was about 50 steps from reaching the outside of the restaurant. Curt had likely come in on purpose to antagonize him. Lord knows he didn't want to go to jail today, but...

"Did I do something wrong, the reason you wanted to speak to me in private?" Curt continued. His voice was so innocent, but Jhalil knew the truth. "Was it me poppin' up yesterday unannounced?"

"Naw. I just have a little headache," Jhalil mumbled. He never turned around and instead, reached for the door handle. "We'll discuss it another day, man."

"Maybe a little sex will help?" Curt inquired and fumbled with his bowtie in the mirror. "I heard sex eases stress, headaches, pain, and all that jazz."

"Oh, yeah?" Jhalil responded dryly, "Have a good day."

"If I had a woman as sexy as Lorraina," Curt said cockily and slowly, "I'd be at home with her now, instead of at a prayer meeting. I mean, with thighs like that, and a booty so round? You could not PAY me to leave that fine piece of tail."

Jhalil whipped around and just knew some hidden camera crew was pranking him. His breath caught in his throat as he attempted to find the best way to handle it. *What would Jesus do?* he asked himself. That thought was short-lived as Curt continued to speak.

"I mean, seriously, bruh. You really thought I came around to help you with your little startup ministry? I just wanted to taste your first lady one last time. She was so good before that I couldn't help myself."

Jesus would have to work a miracle…*now*. Jhalil lost control and forcefully shoved Curt into the mirror, breaking it instantly. Shards of glass flew everywhere as he grabbed Curt's neck with one hand, and then punched him with the other hand. Curt's nose became bloody, and then he took a punch at Jhalil.

"After all I've done, you want to *fight* me?" Curt asked as if he did not realize why Jhalil was so mad. "Bruh, come on! Let me go! You—you broke my nose!"

The door opened behind them, and in rushed another member of the clergy. "Hey! Hey! Cut it out, guys!" The man attempted to break them apart, but their bubbling anger and relentless adrenaline kept the scuffle going.

A worker burst through the doors shortly after. It was a woman who held a phone up to her ear. She screamed at the men who were moving around in the restroom violently. "I've called the police! They're on the way! Stop before you kill yourselves!"

Jhalil was the first to back away and spit his saliva at Curt. Although Curt was much more towering and huskier, Jhalil was quicker on his feet. He shook his sore knuckles out that were beginning to bleed badly, and then he wiped the corner of his nose where he was not sure if it were blood or mucus flowing from it.

"You thought I was going to keep quiet about you wrapping up her panties? I don't care what kind of relationship you used to have with her. You stay away from Lorraina! You stay away from *me*!" Jhalil yelled and kicked Curt a final time.

The once smug man was now lying on the floor in a growing puddle of blood. He looked helpless as he attempted to catch his breath and make sense of the beating his body had just endured. Jhalil limped away and rubbed at his neck. The female worker jumped back in horror.

"You don't need to call the police. Just call a plastic surgeon. He may need his face reconstructed."

Jhalil looked back at Curt a final time and walked out.

When he arrived home, Lorraina had fallen back to sleep on the couch. Their uneaten breakfast was still on the table. A part of him felt horrible for missing out on her delicious home cooking after she slayed over the stove, but the other part of him felt relieved. He had literally beaten and taken his frustrations out on Curt, and it felt good.

He sat down a few feet from Lorraina on the opposite loveseat with his head down. God was likely not pleased with his actions, but he could not help it. Curt had made some over-the-top remarks and it had gotten him a black eye, swollen jaw, and possible broken nose. Jhalil was no longer the spiritual leader with rational thinking. He was the overprotective fiancé looking out for his woman, and he would do it all over again.

Lorraina stirred awake beside him and yawned. As she stretched, she opened her eyes completely and then screamed in shock. She was no doubt surprised to see him sitting there, but was probably also alarmed by his bloody shirt, erratic breathing, and unruly appearance.

"What happened? Are you okay?"

"The better question is: do you forgive me for keeping you waiting?"

"Of course," she said and looked him up and down. Any sleep that had been tugging at her seemed to disappear immediately. "Don't tell me. You got into it with Curt?"

"It was a little discussion, that's all."

"More like a BRAWL! I'm so sorry you felt like you had to defend my honor in this way. Are you sure you're okay? Let me see your face."

"Baby, I'm fine." He dodged her hands when she reached for him. "That guy is an idiot. He won't be bothering you ever again, you hear me?"

She nodded and got up to get him a washcloth. "I hear you. So that's *his* blood?"

"Yeah." Jhalil followed behind her and pulled his shirt off. He tossed it to the hardwood floor and then his voice took on a playful tone. "I'm just ready to shower and eat. Reheat my food, woman, and I'm not going to ask again."

"Whatever you say, Mr. Harrison," she joked, but at the back of her mind, she was upset that he had gotten hurt because of her.

She and her baggage were always coming back to haunt her and the people she loved, and she had the craziest feeling that Curtis was not even close to being finished.

Chapter Nineteen

(Seven months later)

"You must've seen what I was wearing tonight?"

Lorraina looked up from applying lotion to her arms and admired Jhalil's outfit. He wore a getup that matched hers in color and in fabric. They both were dressed to impress and ready for their night on the town. He rocked a cream cashmere pullover, tan slacks, and tan loafers. She also wore a cream blouse, a chocolate brown pencil skirt, and tan and chocolate brown wedge sandals. They were coordinated perfectly.

Earlier in the week, he promised to show her a good time since they had not gotten any alone time lately, and she was anxious to begin their date. They vowed that they would put all the phones, watches, iPods, iPads, and any other distractions away.

Tonight was theirs simply because as of late, life had gotten chaotic but beautiful.

The ministry was officially a thing of the future, and many people were pouring in by the numbers every Sunday and Tuesday evening. It was like the personification of Deuteronomy 30, because God had surely restored everything that was lost, as Jhalil and Lorraina clung more and more to Him.

Jhalil was preaching the Good Word as if he had done it for decades, and Lorraina was his faithful first lady to-be and touching women's lives all over with her testimony. A few of the naysayers loved to turn their nose up at her, given her past. Their relationship was often questioned as well. After all, a male and female heading a church as anything other than a married couple was almost unheard of in the Church of God in Christ realm. Lorraina was determined to move forward despite the doubters and let God handle the rest. She was not going to let those moments define her any longer.

Nothing or no one could stop her spiritual "resurrection," just as nothing or no one could stop the budding love that Jhalil had for her. He had mentioned it again and again about a simple wedding ceremony, but Lorraina was convinced that when the time was right, their nuptials would be in order. There was just so much to be concerned with lately, including providing for their four-year-old foster child, whom they had taken in.

A member of their church—a young, drug-addicted mother—had become overwhelmed and needed help with her son, so Jhalil had volunteered their home temporarily. Lorraina would joke that he favored Jhalil in many ways and ask if he was really the father, but he would only laugh it off.

She could honestly say she never imagined being thrown into motherhood this way, but it was God's Will, and she would stick to it as best as she could. She enjoyed loving and protecting a little person. His name was Noah, and he had the sweetest spirit and temperament she had ever seen from a child. He had been dropped off an hour ago to her best friend, Khloey's, house.

"Maybe. Maybe not," she joked with a wink.

Jhalil approached her with his arms open and she fell into his embrace with a smile. He smelled amazing and looked incredible. He had completely reinvented his look and wore a low-cut now. He had grown out his beard as well, so it was

nice and full now so that each time they kissed, it
tickled her face.

"You ready?"

"I am," she responded and tucked her clutch
purse under an arm.

They were heading to a jazz festival that
took place every year in Dunges Bay Park. Lorraina
was a huge music lover, and Jhalil had played
several instruments as a child. This date would be
one for the books.

He brought along an oversized lawn chair
and a thick fleece blanket that he placed over both
of their shoulders. They had front row seats, and the
show was just getting started as they settled down in
the grass. Lorraina nestled closer to him; she was
half on his lap, and half on the chair. His arm
wrapped around her hips and held her in place.
They enjoyed music and refreshments for more
than an hour before the band took the stage for
their final song. The lead singer of the group
stepped forward and looked around at the crowd.

"Beautiful people, you all are lookin'
GOOD out there! Give it up for yourselves
tonight," he said into the microphone. He was
obviously still stuck in the seventies, judging from
his wardrobe, hairstyle, and lingo. "Y'all ready to
keep groovin'?"

Lorraina smirked and looked around. There
was so much love in the air. There were mainly
couples that had come out tonight. The atmosphere
was different; she could not quite put her finger on
it, but even Jhalil was different. He wore a
continuous smile on his face, and he could not stop
looking at her. She knew she looked great, but his
stare made her feel like the prettiest girl in the
world.

"Before we go any further, from my understanding, I have a friend here tonight who has an important mission. He wants to propose to his girlfriend," the musician continued. "Where are you, buddy?"

Lorraina nudged Jhalil and looked around to see whom the musician was referring to. To her surprise, the spotlight swung around and stopped on them. Lorraina jumped in surprise and felt her mouth go dry. The crowd *ooohed*, and the band played softly while Jhalil cleared his throat and stood up. He brought her along with him and wrapped his arms around her.

"Baby, you already know how I feel about you. You've changed my life and everything in it for the better. I can't live my life without you, and I pray you feel the same," Jhalil spoke sincerely and then released her so that he could get down on one knee.

Lorraina's heart thumped anxiously, dreading the moment and what it meant. She swallowed the lump in her throat while she quickly looked around at everyone and then back at Jhalil. Any other woman would have been ecstatic to be in this position, but she didn't feel good about it at all.

"I did not ask properly the first time around or have the ring to back it up, so I'm asking again in front of these people. Will you please spend the rest of your life with me? Will you marry me, Lorraina?"

The night was young, and romance was in the air. The mood was just right with music and dim lighting, and the love of her life was kneeling before her. This should have been the most beautiful moment of her adult life and certainly the most memorable. Yet she wasn't overjoyed. She wasn't ready to say 'yes,' even though she loved him. She knew she had underlying issues that needed resolving, and there were all kinds of demons that needed to be dismissed from her life once and for all.

She wasn't quite ready to expose the skeletons in her closet. She knew she couldn't embarrass Jhalil in front of all the onlookers, so with tears of frustration in her eyes, she nodded and jumped up and down. She had to take on the role of an excited, unexpected girlfriend.

"Yes! Yes, I will!" she cried and her voice was lack of any emotion or sincerity, but Jhalil did not seem to notice.

The bandleader pumped a fist and then clapped his hands. He reminded Lorraina of the late, great James Brown with his permed hair and leather ensemble. "Let's give it up for this beautiful, young couple! They're headed to the Left Hand Club pretty soon! Woo hoo!" he announced.

The crowd roared with affirmation and excitement. Jhalil smiled and kissed her with passion, while she desperately tried to understand why she was so disconnected and torn about their future. She looked own at her engagement ring—it was perfection wrapped in silver and diamonds.

That night, as they settled in their separate beds, she knew that they were still trying to head down the straight and narrow path. However, she needed a release. There was no one for her to really talk to who would understand her logic, her thinking, or her struggles—not even Jhalil, so she went to her go-to stress reliever.

Buried underneath her sheets, she took out her seven-inch, black sex toy that she kept hidden from Jhalil, and even her closest of friends. She

cried herself to sleep while she pleasured herself,
and cursed her own, cold heart.

Chapter Twenty

The next morning, Lorraina pretended to be asleep for as long as possible, until she was sure that Jhalil had left the house. It was her mission to avoid him as much as possible until she could come up with good reasoning as to why they needed to wait on marriage. Plus, she knew he would be asking her a million different questions, and talking about their wedding, and she was not ready to face him just yet. As she finally pulled herself out of bed, she searched the house for him and instead found a note on the refrigerator.

The brothers and I are meeting at the church. Here's some money to do whatever. See you later, baby. I mean FIANCEE. HAHAHAHA! Love U. -J

She read his note with a saddened heart and admired her ring finger. He had great taste and had picked out a gorgeous ring that fit her style perfectly. But it still just wasn't right. She took the money he left and stashed it in her purse, and then showered and got Noah ready for the day. She would shop away her pain, beginning with retail, and ending with groceries.

More than an hour later, she found herself in the crowded aisles of her favorite grocery store. She spoke aloud to herself about what they needed for the next week and a half. Noah looked at her now with big, bright eyes as he sat in the front part of a shopping cart. He was probably wondering if she had lost her mind. Honey Dijon chicken wraps had been on her mind to make today, so she made sure she had all the ingredients. She picked up things she had no business buying and grabbed more than enough food.

As she headed down one aisle, she baby-talked to Noah. He had a hearing impairment and wore a cochlear implant. He studied her lips, burst into laughter, and then continued to smile at her as she spoke.

"We're just about ready to go. I just need one more thing, okay, man?" she told him and squinted while she read the nutrition label on a can of black beans.

"I didn't know you were a mother."

Lorraina glanced up from the can, startled by the voice. It was Curt. Like all villains to any story, they just had to keep reappearing and making the good people's lives miserable. She sighed and placed the box on the shelf. That was her cue to leave this store.

"There's a lot of things you don't know about me," she said simply.

"It's been almost a year. You should be thankful."

She glanced over a shoulder. "Thankful? And why is that?"

He looked at a can of lima beans, and she knew it was to irk her. There was no way that he could be shopping for those types of beans. No black man in America *willingly* shopped for lima beans.

"I could have pressed charges. I could have gotten your man arrested. I could have done a lot to ruin your name and good graces."

"So, why didn't you?" she challenged and turned completely. "Curt, you don't scare me."

Curt shook his head thoughtfully. He glanced at her body and lingered on her legs. She was dressed modestly in leggings and a lengthy blouse that hung past her buttocks. Even still,

Lorraina felt like he was undressing her with his eyes. Finally, he rubbed the patch of hair along his jawline and then shrugged.

"I'm not trying to. It's all very simple, Lorraina. I really liked you," he spoke seriously. "You *played* me, and I'm not going to lie. It hurt a lot."

"I'm sorry, Curtis. What more do you want me to say? I made a horrible mistake, but I had no idea it would turn into anything more than a good time."

"Just say you'll go out with me tomorrow. Nothing more and nothing less." He held up his hands innocently. "I won't press the issue anymore, and I won't give you a hard time. I won't even come around anymore if you agree to it. Just give me one final night."

"One final night? Please don't do this." She could feel Noah's eyes on her in confusion. He could sense her anxiety as she balled her fists against the cart rail.

"Nothing sexual. Just a simple date," Curt said firmly.

Lorraina could not be too sure if his intentions were good or not. She studied his body language, and he did not seem like he was high off anything but his ego. It unnerved her that she was even considering going with him.

"Why are you doing this?" she asked.

"Just say yes. I promise it's nothing like that. Just…a…simple…date," he repeated as if she had not heard him the first time.

"When? Where?"

Curt smiled as if he had just been gifted the world.

"Meet me at that new restaurant that just opened up downtown. Six thirty. Don't keep me waiting."

"Whatever." She turned away from his smug grin and looked to Noah who was still just as confused about this strange man speaking with his guardian. "You ready to go, baby?"

He nodded, understanding her, and then kicked his little legs in delight. If only he knew what she had foolishly agreed to. Now she had to figure out what she was going to tell Jhalil tomorrow. In a matter of seconds, her life had gotten that much more complicated, and she hated herself for even doing something so stupid.

***

The next evening, Lorraina was a ball of nerves as 6:00 rolled around. It was time to head out and meet Curt at the destination he chose. She had never heard of this restaurant, but there were rave reviews about it online. It was situated in the middle of other thriving businesses and looked to be bustling with food connoisseurs. She made up a lie to tell to Jhalil, and he surprisingly was nonchalant about her request to have a night out with the girls. He even told her to stay out "as long as possible."

That was odd. He usually reprimanded her for hanging out with her friends because of their pasts. She was the only one of her crew to turn her life around so he wanted her to stay as far away as she could from those women. He especially wanted her to be careful now that she was representing his ministry. But tonight, something was different about him.

Lorraina eased the ruby-colored dress up her hips and then turned with her back to him to zip.

"You look incredible. Is this new?"

"No. You've just never seen it before."

"And where did you say you were going again?"

"The lounge on Fourth Street—Mickey's," she lied. She would actually be four blocks down from that lounge, but he couldn't know that.

"Have fun and please be careful." He studied the side of her face. Worry was etched all over her expression, so he just had to ask. "Is something wrong?"

Lorraina said nothing and concentrated on smoothing down the tiny hairs along her forehead. She wore a simple ponytail that had been fluffed with a comb to give her extra volume. On her lips was a nude-colored lipstick that brought out the yellow undertones in her skin. She felt attractive, but all for the wrong reasons. There were no true motives as to why she was going out with a man who could ruin everything for her with a simple phone call.

She arrived at the restaurant without successfully talking herself out of the foolishness. "Hi, I am here for…"

The hostess interrupted her words. "Ah, yes. The gentleman informed us that you would be arriving shortly. Right this way, Miss."

Lorraina followed the petite Asian woman to the back of the restaurant. A private room awaited her, which she was grateful for. This meant that they would be hidden from view from any nosey onlookers. She could not afford to be caught dining out with anyone other than Jhalil, and certainly not with Curt. That would be a bad look altogether.

He was nowhere in sight as she settled in one of the loveseats and exhaled.

"Why did I agree to this?" she questioned aloud.

There was an uneasy feeling in her heart that she could not shake. There was no telling what kind of game Curt was playing but she knew that she was desperate for some kind of resolution. If having dinner with him helped her get rid of him from here on out, then she would be satisfied.

She waited 14 minutes exactly before declaring that her time was wasted. But as she stood up and reached for her handbag, another hand closed around her wrist.

"You leavin' *already*?" a voice pondered with sarcasm.

The warmth of Curt's breath tickled the tiny hairs at the back of her neck. A chill ran down her spine and seemed to run throughout her body. Finally, the chill went to her feet where her toes curled, but not in a good way. She faced him and was shocked to find that they were not the only two in the room. Two other men, dressed in black suits, accompanied Curt. They wore black shades and earpieces as if they were a part of the Secret Service.

"What is *this*?"

He noticed her unsettled expression and held up his hands. "Calm down. Calm down. These are just a couple friends of mine, Emilio and Julio. We're here to talk with you and enjoy a little Italian cuisine. We're not trying to start any trouble, okay?"

She was still unsure about all of this; the way Emilio looked at her up and down unnerved her. Even behind his dark-colored shades, she had managed to capture his attention. Perhaps she should not have worn such a revealing, form fitting dress. The men practically *searched* through the material of her dress for skin and whatever else they could find.

As she reluctantly sat back down, she breathed out a deep exhale. Whatever was to become of this night, she did not necessarily care. She simply wanted everything to be over so she could head back home to relax in her warm bed.

"I'm glad you came with me today. I promise I won't keep you out all night, and I won't be inappropriate."

Lorraina studied his face. She looked at his slightly twisted nose that Jhalil had broken so many months prior. He seemed genuine in his statements. She spoke over the soft music overhead, "Well, I appreciate that."

"What will you be having?" Curt asked and peered over his menu at her.

She shrugged. "I'm not even sure. I'm not a big Italian fan."

"Word? That's news to my ears. So, what do you normally eat?"

"Anything that comes from my own kitchen," she joked. "Soul food...Creole dishes...Jamaican cuisine."

He nodded thoughtfully. "You cook?"

"Why is that so surprising? Most women *do*, don't they?"

"Not the ones I've dated," he admitted and rubbed the patch of hair along his jawline. "It's like pulling teeth with some of these twenty-first century women. They don't want to cook, clean, work, or anything else. They just want a man to do it all, and expect him not to tire out. *Please.*"

"What kind of women were YOU dating?" Lorraina chuckled and placed her menu down beside her on the table. "All of the women in my family and around me were brought up with totally different views. But hey, to each her own."

The waitress came around and took their orders. Emilio and Julio sat at the opposite end of the table and conversed amongst themselves. She was content because that made things a little less awkward.

"If you don't mind me asking," he began to say, but she cut him off.

"I mind. Anytime somebody starts a sentence like that, it's a personal question."

Curt laughed and looked surprised at her wittiness. "It's not like that. Well, it is, but you don't have to answer if you don't want." He paused and looked her directly in the eye. "Are you in love with Jhalil?"

Lorraina swallowed hard. On one hand, she could be honest with him because he genuinely seemed interested. On the other hand, she was unsure of where this information would be used.

"Why do you want to know?"

"I'm just curious."

"What? You're going to run and tell him what I say? Who's benefitting from this piece of information?"

"My goodness. *Chill.* You're so defensive, Lo Lo. I'm merely just making conversation. Didn't I say I didn't want to start any trouble with you? I only wanted to have a nice dinner where we could talk."

"First of all, do *not* call me Lo Lo, and two, yes I love him. He knows that already."

Curt shrugged and nodded. "See? That wasn't so bad, was it? That's all I wanted to know."

Lorraina continued to stare at him. Things grew quiet but she kept her gaze on him, even while the waitress came with their plates and placed them on the table. The food looked delicious and steamed from the oven still. Only when her mouth began to water at the aromas of flavor did she look away from him.

"What now? I know that wasn't all you wanted to know. Don't play with me."

"No one's playing with you...this time," Curt paused, and a snide smile tugged at the corners of his mouth. She could slap it off. "Now, more than a year ago? I played with you in more ways than one. That was a playground that I would not mind frequenting again."

It was obvious that he was referring to her body, and the few times that they had fooled around. She sighed because she knew the shaming and name-calling would be next. This was probably his plan all along.

"Okay, you know what? You're crossing the line!" Her voice rose as she stood to her feet for the second time. Her napkin fell to the floor from her lap. "I'm leaving!"

"You might not want to do that." His voice was controlled and low. He never faltered as he leaned to bite into his chicken and pasta. "You might see something you don't like."

"Oh, like seeing you is any better? What can be worse? Goodbye, Curt...for good. I don't care what you do from here on out. I can't put myself through this anymore."

"Okay. Go ahead, sweetheart."

Lorraina snatched her bag from the table and stepped through the doors separating the private room from the restaurant's main seating area. She mumbled under her breath in irritation and half expected Curt to come up behind her to try to stop her. But he never came. Instead, she was stopped literally in her tracks at the sight of Jhalil, who had encouraged her to stay out late and have a good time, seated in the corner of the restaurant.

Her handbag dropped with a gentle thud, and her knees seemed to lock in place. She was not upset because he was out having dinner nor was she mad that he wanted to enjoy himself and dress up with a suit and tie. What upset her was that Jhalil was out having dinner, dressed like a GQ model, and sitting across from another woman.

This bastard was cheating while she tried desperately to save her family from Curt's foolish games.

Chapter Twenty-One

Jhalil chuckled and grabbed the cloth napkin from the table as Lorraina continued to look on in shock. He seemed genuinely happy and then reached over to wipe the young woman's face free of pasta sauce. Her heart sank a little more in her chest; it was nearly on top of her feet. The two literally looked like a couple in love.

The woman, from what Lorraina could see, was attractive and petite with a honey-brown complexion. Her smooth skin was free of any makeup, except for the light splash of blush. Either it was literal blush on her cheeks, or Jhalil had her blushing nonstop. She could not decipher. Lorraina's perusal took in the woman's wardrobe next. She wore a simple black dress, fishnet stockings with bows on the backs of each ankle, and black kitten heels. Lastly, her thick hair was naturally curly and pinned up intricately. The woman was stunning.

"What...what did you do, Jhalil?" she asked under her breath.

Tears brimmed her eyes. She vowed that she would not make a scene, nor would she allow the tears to fall from her eyes. She blinked away the feeling of despair that crept into her veins. She was being cheated on with a man she loved and wanted to *someday* marry. It was truly the slap of the century.

As she turned to leave the restaurant, a hand closed around her wrist and stopped her in her tracks for a second time that night. She looked up at Curt who had a knowing look on his face. Was this the very thing that he was trying to stop her from seeing? He seemed concerned by the tears welling up in her eyes, and pulled her into his arms. He leaned to kiss the top of her head, and then ushered them in the opposite direction and away from Jhalil's line of view.

"What is that? You KNEW about this?"

"*Shhh*. Sit down. Let me talk to you for a second," Curt said and pulled the chair out for her. Only after she sat down did he continue to talk. "I didn't want you to find out this way."

"That's a load of crap and you know it, Curt. Why else would you invite me here? You knew he was coming here for whatever reason, and you wanted me to find out. I'm going to ask for the last time before I leave—what kind of game are you playing?"

"I'm not playing *any* game. I promise you, sweetheart. I was only trying to open your eyes to what Jhalil is really about," he said and then looked around. "Hey, Emilio! Julio!"

The two burly men walked over. "Yeah, boss?"

"Tell her what I do for a living."

They looked at Curt, then to each other, and then back to Curt again. Emilio spoke up this time. There was hesitation in his voice.

"For real, *for real?*"

"Yes. For real, *for real*. We can trust that she won't say a thing. Isn't that right, Lorraina?"

She nodded in confusion and looked back and forth between the three. When she spoke, her voice was raspy with terror, "Your secret's safe with me but…but what's going on?"

Emilio cleared his throat and crossed his arms. "We're all undercover special agents."

"What? I didn't do anything…" she began to protest with her hands up.

"No, no. It's not *you* we're looking out for," Curtis assured her and kept his voice low. He nodded towards the outside of the restaurant. "It's Jhalil who we've been pursuing for a few years."

This was all a shock to Lorraina as she gripped a hand over her chest. She could feel her world tilt. "A few YEARS? For *what?*"

"We have reason to believe he's been participating in a major sex trafficking stint we've been investigating."

Now, it was time for her to *really* gasp and find the ability to breathe properly. If she had not been sitting, she would have surely fallen backward. She could not believe what she was hearing.

"Please tell me this is an unfunny, sick, and long, drawn-out joke."

Emilio and Julio dismissed themselves.

"I wish I could," Curt said. "There was no other way for me to tell you, but to tell you the truth. Now, I could totally lose my job over this— Emilio and Julio included. But we're trusting that you would help us to move this assignment further. Not only that, but I cared about you enough to show you what your man *really* thought of you. He's a clown, Lorraina, and you deserve better."

"Look, all past mistakes and past relations aside. Why should I believe you? Why should I trust what you're saying? Why should I believe that this is what's really going on, and he's not just cheating on me?"

"Because of this," Curt said simply and handed her a thick, manila envelope.

She reluctantly opened the envelope with shaky hands. Much to her surprise, tucked deep in the contents of the material were countless identification cards with Jhalil's face plastered on each one. Each card had a different name and state of residence on it. It was like the movie starring Leonardo DiCaprio, where he had posed as many different people in various professions.

Her mouth ran dry. "I—I…this…doesn't…oh, my goodness," she stuttered.

Her eyes met Curt's in disbelief. She had fallen in love with a con artist. This made no sense. Why did she have to be at the short end of the stick? Why did her heart have to be broken in this way? Perhaps it was God punishing her for all her previous dirty deeds that she had committed while serving in the ministry. As the saying went, God didn't like ugly, and this was proof that she had been rebuked because of her sins.

"Bu—but how? Why? Why would he do this?"

Curt tapped his index finger against his temple. "The mind of a criminal is a complicated one, sweetheart. All I can say is he's looking for something, whether it's love, affection, power, or control. Many of the men who seek out these women are often abusive, aggressive, and charming. Has he ever put his hands on you?"

This was a no-brainer. "Well, no, but…"

"Has he ever pressured you into anything you didn't want to do?"

"Honestly, I can't say he has."

Curt nodded. "Well, you're one of the lucky ones. It's possible he does care for you, but he can't let go of the other things he's gotten himself into it. The money in this industry is addicting; it's like a drug."

Lorraina shook her head in incredulity. "So, when are you guys going to bust him? How does all of this work?"

"Only when we have sufficient evidence can we start making arrests. Until then, it's been a waiting game. We don't want to just go in for the kill and not have all the proper resources. That not only puts our operations at risk, but the women involved as well."

Lorraina nodded, understanding. She felt like she had been caught on a TV show and was being pranked. But this was real. The photos and evidence were real. Jhalil's double life was real. Curt and his motives were real.

"I think I'm going to be sick," she whispered.

He sat back for a minute, allowing her to fan herself and calm down.

"That's why we need *you*," he continued, handing her a glass of water and napkin. "I have exhausted all of my options, and while it's pretty much against federal regulations to get a regular civilian involved, there is something about you."

Lorraina stared back at him in silence.

"You're able to get people to open up and trust every word that falls from those pretty lips. You're able to make the strongest of men fall to their knees. That's how you got me to fall so hard for you," Curt added.

Even though she was distraught because of the news she had found out, her heart warmed at his words. Maybe he wasn't so crazy after all.

"You know that cutie, Noah?"

"Of course."

"Noah is the son of one of the ladies he recently met. That's another tactic for these bastards. They take the women's children and bribe them with a better life, knowing the women will do any and everything to provide for their children. This was all intentional on Jhalil's behalf."

"But she joined our church."

"Okay, and look who's leading it?"

Curt had a point.

"So, tell me something. That day we met at church…" she began to speak softly, but he held up his index finger.

"Go home now. They've received dessert, so he'll probably be leaving with the young lady, and I don't want you to run into him. Head out the back way. One of my agents will escort you. I'll be talking with you more soon, okay?"

Lorraina nodded and was still in a shock. "Okay. Thank you for this."

"Absolutely. Be safe. Keep your eyes and ears open, you hear?"

She nodded and then turned away to leave. A piece of her heart stayed right there in the restaurant as she headed home, showered, and then buried herself in her bed. Jhalil came home hours later. He settled in bed in the room next to her, and she pretended to be asleep while masking her tears in her pillows.

Life had truly been turned upside down.

Chapter Twenty-Two

It was hard for Lorraina to push past the details that Curt had broken down to her, but she made a vow that if not for these women, she would fight to free Noah. Sex trafficking prevention was always something that she was passionate about. Even though she used her body willingly to lure men into her bedroom once upon a time, this was an entirely different ballpark. She had done it for satisfaction and pleasure, whereas the women affected by sex trafficking were often tricked into the lifestyle. These women were blindsided by their companions; they were promised false hopes of riches and fulfilled dreams. This was not fair to any woman caught up in the sex trade. Lorraina vowed to do whatever it took to get Jhalil the consequences he deserved.

She was also saddened that the love of her life was leading a double life. She was sad that forever would not include them, and she was sad that she had not seen the signs earlier. But now it all made sense. Jhalil would come home with wads of money saying it was a love offering from different speaking engagements. He would always take a change of clothes with him to his outings. He would be skeptical about her accompanying him to special events. Why was she so blind to this before?

Curt was helpful in this journey. He spoke with her on many occasions, offering support, and apologizing for Jhalil's actions although it was far from his fault. She appreciated him being honest with her, just as she thanked him for opening up to her.

"How are you holding up otherwise?"

They were on the phone currently. She shrugged as if he could see her, saying, "I'm okay. I'm a little heartbroken, but I'm going to get through it like I always do."

"That's understandable. This is a man you trusted and loved. It's not going to be easy, but just from the few conversations I have had over the last several months with you, I know that you're one tough cookie. Hard interior, soft inside, and well put together."

"That was the worst analogy ever," Lorraina chuckled.

"Yeah. I couldn't backtrack once I started speaking," Curt agreed with a laugh. "What, um…what are you doing later?"

Lorraina looked over at Noah who was asleep. "I have no plans as usual."

"Is Jhalil going to be around?"

"I honestly haven't kept up with him anymore. I'm just so completely turned off from him. We've been arguing like crazy lately, and I'm so tempted to leave. If it weren't for getting Noah out of this situation, then I would have already left. He goes his way, and I go my way."

While local agents continued their investigation, she had to pretend that everything was okay. She had to smile in his face, ward off his marriage talk as politely as possible, and keep a cool head. It was hard, to say the least. There was so much tension in the house that she could literally slice the air with a knife. Until recently, she could not fathom the thought of losing him, but now she had no choice.

"Maybe I can take you out?"

She did not hesitate. "Sure. I'll drop Noah off to my friend's house."

"You were going to ask me something in the restaurant about when I first met with you. Do you remember what that was?"

Lorraina closed her eyes. "It's never left my mind. I just have to know, and please, be honest with me."

"What's wrong?"

"The day you met me in church; did you know what Jhalil was doing then?"

"I knew what Jhalil was doing, yes. Like I said, we've been investigating him for a couple of years now. Did I know you two were together or had any ties? *No.* I was at church, enjoying service, and couldn't keep my eyes off you. That was no mistake. That's what complicated things once we met again. I had to put up this front and be rude to you all, and act like I was a jerk just to save face. I was happy to be reuniting with you. I can't tell you enough how attracted I was to you, so it was a blow when I found out you were dealing with him."

"How can you like someone so much that you've only met with a couple times?" she questioned.

"What's there *not* to like about you? You are educated, well put together, and beautiful. Like I said, when I came to your church, I was looking for a place to worship, honest to God. But then my mind went other places when I saw you sitting up there with your legs crossed. The light hit your face just right; I was nearly in love!"

"Wow."

"Yeah. I'm not trying to make you uncomfortable, but it was more than sex for me. Those few times we met, we talked about everything under the sun. I never believed in love at first sight, but by our fifth date, or whatever you want to call it, I really cared for you."

"This is absolutely crazy," Lorraina muttered to herself.

She could feel her joy seeping away more and more, just as she could feel her heart breaking. All this time, she thought Curt was an idiot who wanted to destroy her reputation, relationship, and integrity, but his mission was the opposite. He was only doing those things to get as far as he could with solving the madness that Jhalil had created. She had treated him so badly. Jhalil had even fought with him.

They went to a restaurant and picked up the conversation where it had been left off.

"So where do we go from here?"

"Well, Jhalil's day is coming. I would say…"

"No, not with him. I'm talking about with us?"

"There can't be an us, can there? Certainly, with your line of work and with my involvement to Jhalil, it would never work."

"Never say never," he whispered with a wink. "As for Jhalil, my team and I are trying to hold out for another month or so. He and I will be meeting and I'm going to try to get him to confess. However, with or without the confession, we will likely have enough evidence to incriminate him by then."

"There's no way he's going to meet with you."

"Oh, but he will." He smiled. "Especially if I have money and women for him."

"What do you mean?"

"I'm going to bring in a couple of female officers who will pose as helpless women. We seem to have picked up on his preference. Tall, almost lanky women with light hair and petite bodies are what he's been seen with, other than the young lady we saw at the restaurant."

"How many would you say?" she asked, but truthfully, she didn't want to know. She wasn't sure her heart could take it.

Curt thought for a moment. "Are you sure you want to know?"

"Tell me," she begged.

"More than a dozen children, and close to 32 women."

Lorraina grew sick to her stomach right then and there. She held a hand over her mouth, but it was too late. She threw up all over the place and ran to the nearest restroom. She was sure that all attraction for her had left Curt's mind. She was a mess…literally. All eyes were on her from the other women in the restroom.

"Oh, God! Help me. This…this can't be right. This man helped me through my darkest hour. I prayed for him! How can he be this monster?" she asked aloud.

She was glad that all the women had run off in confusion because she dropped to her knees in the stall and prayed right then and there. Never mind that it was an unsanitary place to be on her knees, she needed God right then and there. Then, after cleaning herself up, she splashed cold water on her face and looked at her image in the mirror.

She shook her head leisurely and still could not seem to wrap her mind around what had taken place. She figured this was God's punishment for all her sins so long ago. It was either that, or she was living out one of the longest nightmares of her life.

"Just show me the truth, God. Please reveal Yourself to me."

As the words touched the atmosphere, two women walked into the restroom wearing dresses that were so short and revealing that they would make strippers blush. Their high heels clicked rhythmically against the tile, and they both settled before the mirror behind her to freshen up their lipstick.

The slimmer of the two was the first to speak. "Robyn, did you see what he had in that briefcase?"

The blonde-haired woman spoke up, "No, I didn't. What was it? He opened and closed it so quickly that I missed it."

"Giiiirl, stacks and stacks of money. That man is paid!"

"Does he think we're some kind of prostitutes or something?"

"Uh, HELLO? We are, dummy!"

"Oh, yeah! Aye, regardless, Momma needs to pay the rent," the woman joked and pushed her breasts up suggestively. "Plus, he knows he's a cutie."

"He's all right. Jhalil looks *waaaay* better."

Lorraina's hands paused against the paper towel that she was using. Had this woman really said Jhalil? It wasn't too often that you heard that name, so it had to be *her* Jhalil. Lorraina looked at the women from head to feet. She took in their appearances, pieced their conversation together, and then whipped around.

"Stay far away from him."

"Huh?" Both women turned around in confusion. "You're talking to us?"

"Yes. You're here with someone named Jhalil, you said? He's brown skinned with a full beard, and on his forearm are multiple tattoos. Am I right?"

The two women looked at each other as the blonde began to talk. "Uh, yeah. That's *definitely* him. He's our date for tonight. Who are you? His wife? I swear he didn't tell us he was married! Isn't that right, Anastasia? Tell her!"

"I'm his fiancée, but that's not even my concern. My concern is that he's been involved in the sex trafficking industry and I'm trying to stop you two from falling into one of his traps. He's tricked over 30 women and several children as well. I don't want you to be the next victims."

"Are you serious right now?"

"I would not lie to you. He's under investigation as we speak. I'm here with an undercover detective now. It's best you ladies leave now. Find a backway or a side exit, but do not stop and talk to him. All he wants is your bodies and pretty faces for money. That money is for his partner to 'purchase' your freedom, so to speak. He has no idea I know everything, and he has no idea about the investigation."

Both women looked alarmed, as they nodded, picked up their handbags, and then scurried out of the restroom. Lorraina followed behind cautiously and peeked out into the restaurant. She could not see Jhalil, but she knew he was near. It was like his cologne was in the air. She returned to their table where Curt still sat and then told him what had happened.

"Did you get their names?"

"I only got their first names, Anastasia and Robyn."

"That's good enough." Curt looked around the room and then jotted the information down in his notebook. "Are you okay, by the way? Did something disagree with your stomach?"

"No, I was just overcome with emotion. That's all," she spoke hurriedly as she perused the area. "Can we leave? I don't want to chance him seeing us."

"Sure thing."

The two left and Curt dropped her back off to her home.

Chapter Twenty-Three

Jhalil stood up from the booth he was seated in and walked closer to the window. Was that who he thought it was? The shape of the butt, build of the legs, and even the sway of the hips all pointed to his girlfriend. He dialed Lorraina's number but the woman he was staring down never picked up.

Instead, she grabbed the man's arm that she was walking with and nestled her head against his arm. He could have sworn that was Curt and Lorraina leaving out, but obviously it wasn't. He had left her more than two hours ago to tend to business and she was asleep, so he had to have been tripping.

He turned back to the deacon that had come along with him and motioned towards the women's restroom. "Have you seen either of them leave out?"

"No, I can't say that I have, Pastor. I hope they didn't get the wrong idea."

"I hope not either. Maybe the money threw them off."

"Who knows?"

"If only they knew that I was going to pay them to stay off of the streets and get healthy," Jhalil sighed. "This mission has been hard, man. I can't even lie."

"Aren't all missions tough when you're working for Christ?"

"Yeah, but this one especially is difficult because I want to save as many women and children as possible, but there's no real support. How many pastors do you know that are out on the streets, putting their lives on the line, and getting victims of sex crimes the resources they need? How many pastors actually do the *real* work anymore? I just see them in the pulpits, reaping the benefits of a church salary, driving expensive sports cars, and living in their lavish homes."

"I hear you, Pastor. I definitely hear you," Irvin, the long-time friend of Jhalil's, commented. "I meant to ask, have you told Lorraina about this?"

"Not yet. I'm actually afraid to."

"You? Afraid?" he chuckled.

"It's a couple different aspects. She could end up jealous, or she could be very turned off by this mission. I mean, it's a lot to take in. Her man is posing as a pimp, for lack of better words. It's something I've always been passionate about, but I've never had the courage to tell any of the women I was in a relationship with. Even when I was on the streets and didn't have a title in the church, I would do this on the weekends. Whether one life was saved, or 50 lives were saved, it didn't matter to me."

Irvin clapped hands with Jhalil in support. "That's awesome, man. I'm proud of you. But what I'll say to the Lorraina situation is if she truly loves and cares for you like I believe, then she will be open to helping you in this mission. She will support you as well. All you have to do is just sit down and lay everything out on the table. You need to do this especially since you're trying to marry her."

"Yeah, you're absolutely right," Jhalil agreed. "I'll go for it tonight."

As Jhalil decided that the two women were lost causes and loaded up his belongings into the car, a twinge of regret and fear entered his heart. There was no telling how Lorraina would take this news, but if he knew her, then he knew she would be understanding and may even want to participate.

183

So often, she would go around and minister to other young ladies about her promiscuous past, so surely, this would not be any different, right?

He remembered a time where he was first introduced to this world—he was only a teenager. It had hurt his heart when he understood just what was taking place, but he vowed from that moment on that he would dedicate his time and life to rescuing women and children in those situations.

"Sweetheart, your total is $3.56. You are so handsome, by the way."

Jhalil smiled at the middle-aged cashier politely and reached into his back pocket for his wallet. "Thank you, ma'am."

As he pulled out a five-dollar bill, he heard a loud commotion in the aisle next to the checkout area and jumped in shock. The cashier yelled with surprise and then peeked around the cash register to see what was taking place. Items from most of the shelves flew to the floor, grunts could be heard, and the sounds of a woman whimpering were evident.

"What in the world?" he spoke to himself, but his attention was on the unusual noise.

A piece of him knew what was already going on. From the looks of it, a woman was being beaten by her lover. He wanted to help. However, the other part of him knew he didn't have any backup or weapon on him should anything get too crazy. Still, the gentleman in him was concerned.

As he paid the cashier and told her to keep the change, he snatched his plastic bag from the counter and rounded the aisle.

"Hey!" he called out. "Cut it out!"

Sure enough, there was a scrawny man bent over with his pants half hanging down. The man wore boots that slammed into a girl, no older than Jhalil. She was coughing up blood and crying silent tears, but as her eyes opened, they landed on *Jhalil. She seemed to whisper, "help me" even in the midst of her moans.*

Jhalil prayed that everything ended well and went for it. He would be less of a man if he didn't do anything to stop this coward. With all his might, he lunged for the man's waist and brought him down on the floor with him. Jhalil subdued the man's erratic motions by putting all his weight on the guy's ribcage, and then looking over a shoulder.

The young girl was now foaming and bleeding at the mouth, and her body shook uncontrollably. His heart dropped as he cried out, "Somebody, anybody—call the police! Call 911!"

The cashier ran to call for help, while Jhalil continued to restrain the guy. More than 30 minutes later, he was sitting in the waiting room of the hospital where the teenager had been taken for her injuries. She was recovering well, but he wanted to wait to actually see her face before he could breathe again.

A nurse peeked from beyond the curtains of the room, and motioned him over. "Kin of Rita Canales?"

"Friend," he corrected solemnly. "How's she doing?"

"As well as expected. You may visit her for a few minutes before the doctor does his final checkup."

Jhalil escaped his daydream and remembered how he had gotten to know her in just under 15 minutes. He reprimanded her initially for dating someone so much older and classless, but it turned out, she had been separated from her recently deported family and had been his moneymaker for the last several years. He used and abused her body for his own twisted pleasure, and then sold it to other sick men who were willing to lay down with a 17-year-old.

For years, they remained good friends, up until her death. She had full-blown AIDS from a lifestyle that she had not even asked for. It disgusted him that grown men participated in such nonsense. It sickened him that Rita was just one of hundreds of thousands of women who had no choice but to succumb to the misfortunes of sex trafficking. That was where his mission began.

Jhalil finally mustered up the courage in his car to talk to Lorraina, after a quick prayer. But to his dismay, when he rounded the corner of the bedroom, she was gone. Every single one of her belongings was missing. Perplexed, he raced around the room to find anything—any traces of a note or sign that she was coming back. He stumbled upon a hand-written note that read:

I know EVERYTHING. You're SICK and need HELP! Goodbye, Jhalil.

"No, no, no…" he read the note repeatedly, and the only thing he could say was, "*No!*"

He dropped to his knees in a heap of tears. The paper floated to the ground like a feather and joined him on the floor. The very thing he did not want to happen had occurred, and he only had himself to blame. There was no way she knew what was really going on, because if she had, she would not have left him like this. When Lorraina fled, she had taken a part of his heart too because as he wept with confusion, his heart broke more and more.

***

Meanwhile, across town…

"Noah, stay over here, honey," Lorraina spoke as she signed to the child.

She sat cross-legged in the middle of a park she had randomly passed after packing up and leaving her home she shared with Jhalil.

The bench was rickety, the wind nipped at her ankles, and her hair blew out of control, but she felt free. For the first time in weeks, she was content and not worried about her next move. All of the foolishness surrounding Jhalil and his ungodly deeds had her stressed once upon a time, but she felt happy now to have left him.

The decision to separate herself was scary but necessary, and the piles of clothes and belongings in her car was proof that she had followed her heart.

Noah played happily in the sandbox, and she knew she would probably regret allowing him to submerge himself. She was sure cleaning him up would be a task. But she would give him the world if it meant seeing that big smile on his face. Her future as his foster mother was shaky, and she did not know what Jhalil would do once he sought revenge. So, all she could do now was enjoy moments like this.

"It's like I'm baptized in your seduction," a voice declared in the wind.

Lorraina's eyebrows furrowed as she continued staring ahead. The baritone was familiar and caused her insides to quiver, but not in a good way. She knew exactly whom it was before turning around. It was someone she did not have the strength to face not now and not ever. It was a constant face from her past, and one she wanted to keep there. *Capri*.

"What did you say to me?"

"You're still so doggone fine. Dang, girl! What are you, sipping from the fountain of youth or something?"

Lorraina swallowed hard, but not out of fear or anything. She was already irritated by his choice of words and the look in his eyes. She turned back around and pretended that he was not behind her. There was absolutely no way that he was still hung up on their affairs from years back.

"Oh, so you're going to tune me out? I guess you were always good at that."

She turned and finally acknowledged him with a scowl. "Yeah, and you were always good at being CRAZY. What are you doing here?"

"It's a free, public park, last I checked. Why can't I be here, enjoying the weather, like you? I literally was taking a walk and saw the back of your head. Plus, I know that body any time of day."

He settled on the opposite end of the bench where she was seated. In his hand was a cigarette that he lit up with a few flicks of the thumb across his neon lighter. Leisurely, he sucked from the cancer stick with his full lips, and then blew a line of smoke in her face. She fanned it away, coughing, and then began to gather her belongings.

"Leaving so soon? I was just about to give you a piece of my mind," he taunted.

"Haven't you done that enough already?"

He did not answer her. He only stared her down and then shook his head thoughtfully. "I used to LIVE for you. Most importantly, I used to love you, but you played with my heart, Rain. You owe me that much to sit and talk."

She was silent as she settled back on the bench.

"I wanted to marry you once upon a time. I thought you could do or say no wrong. You were my everything, sweetheart. I don't even think you realize what kind of power you had over me," he commented and then gave his cigarette a long draw again.

"What we had was temporary, and it gave us the high we were searching for at that time. But marriage? You know we would have never worked, whether I was leading in the ministry or not," she said gently. "We just weren't meant to be, and it's time you accept that."

Capri slid over on the bench. His hand cupped the back of her neck, and he caressed the side of her face with his thumb. Then his fingers dropped to her neckline, slid over the curve of her breasts, and then landed in her lap. His large hand closed around her thigh before he squeezed it suggestively.

Lorraina pushed his arm away in disgust. "Stop it!"

"You can't say you don't miss what we had."

"I'll say it again and again because I *don't*. I'm a CHANGED woman," she affirmed.

"Yeah, okay," he chuckled. He continued to speak, referring to what she had told him earlier. "But you're right. We would have never worked out. It took me, leaving my wife, to see what I had all along. I mean, let's face it, you were incredible in bed, and I'll never forget what you did for me, but I want my wife back. It had to have been God that led me to see you today."

"Your *wife*?" Lorraina's eyes narrowed in confusion.

"Of course. My wife. Have you heard from Kylie? I haven't seen her since the day we separated at your office."

Lorraina paused and could feel her heart drop. "Are you...*serious*? You really don't know?"

"Know what?" Capri was obviously perplexed.

"Kylie's dead. She...she was shot and killed by police." The words still sounded weird rolling off her tongue.

Capri's already fair complexion seemed to turn even paler as he paused with the cigarette hanging from his mouth. He studied her facial expressions and saw that she was serious. Only a single tear welled up in his left eye and then spilled over onto his cheek.

"What do you mean, *she's dead*? When did this happen? H—how did it happen? Why did they KILL her? She never hurt anybody! Why didn't anyone call me?"

Capri had a million and one questions, and Lorraina only had a few answers. She shrugged on her cardigan and called for Noah. As he turned around and headed for her, she answered Capri solemnly.

"We killed her. Our affair killed her. And truth be told, this conversation is killing my peace. Goodbye, Capri. *Please*...get help."

With that, she propped Noah on her hip, and then turned around and walked away. Capri yelled out in agony, but Lorraina faced forward to avoid growing emotional again. She had cried her last tears over her deceased friend. In a sense, their actions of being secret lovers had not literally killed her, but it had led her to confront Lorraina

190

irrationally with a gun, which led to her untimely demise.

Lorraina situated Noah in his car seat, and then headed for a place she knew would be safest. She drove and did not stop until she reached Curt's home.

"I was hoping you came through. I got your text this morning. Are you okay?"

He spoke lowly as he opened the door with a T-shirt and a pair of joggers on. She swallowed hard and entered cautiously. The way he leaned into the doorframe with power and authority unnerved her. Beneath his clothes, it was obvious he was one of those thick fellas; he had meat on him, but he wasn't fat. He was muscular, but not ridiculous. He was firm but a teddy bear as well.

"I'm fine…*now*," she answered him as she situated Noah in a spare bedroom.

"Did something happen?"

"No, just…just hug me."

Lorraina fell into his embrace and Curt held her as she requested. He moved them to the living room, helped her disrobe from her coat and shoes, and whispered encouraging words to her.

Curt caressed the middle of her back and then slid his hand under her shirt to unlatch her bra strap with one flick of his wrist. She protested and put out her hand.

"No. Please don't," she spoke softly.

"Shhh. You're so tense. Let me take your mind away from what he did," he declared while his hands ran over her shoulders, and he attempted to massage her.

She shook her head again. "No, really. I'm fine, Curt. I just need a shower and *sleep*."

He held his hands up. "I'm not going to force you to do anything. But it's obvious you're hurting right now and can't focus on anything but Jhalil. You keep thinking about his actions and hoping that you're dreaming. But each day that you wake, you realize this is serious, and he really did betray you. You also realize that you wasted your time and love on yet another fool—and that eats you up inside. But what do I know?" he questioned nonchalantly.

Clearly, he was enjoying making her uncomfortable. His words struck her heartstrings harshly. He was right. She hated to admit it, but Jhalil was consuming her every thought as of late. Even in her sleep, she was being disturbed with images of his smile and memories of his precious hugs and love. How could this be? She was still in shock from the first day that his secrets had come out.

Tears sprang to her eyes like a faucet, but she would not dare let Curt see her so vulnerable and broken. On the other hand, she felt safe. Perhaps he cared a lot for her because he soon offered his arms to her. She hugged him and nestled her face in the crook of his neck. His hands did not hesitate in resting along the small of her back.

"It's just so unfair," she wept.

"I know, sweetheart. It seems like the world hands its toughest battles to the most good-hearted people. You didn't deserve any of it," Curt pointed out. "I mean, seriously. If I had a woman like you, I would never leave home."

"Stop it," she snickered. "I'm sorry for wetting up your clothes."

"Don't apologize, and I was totally serious. Why would I need to look somewhere else for something I already have? You're beautiful inside and out, and it's a shame Jhalil could not see that."

"Thank you, Cu—" As she thanked him, he covered her mouth with his.

But unlike any other time, Lorraina did not push him away. Lorraina felt some type of way. It was like she was drawn back into her old ways. She could feel her body cry out and take over her senses and inhibitions. Her broken heart and her mixed emotions caused her to end up naked and in the arms of Curt. He kissed her passionately while she protested not as much as she should have.

She knew God was looking down from the Heavens with disappointment, just as her heart cried out in frustration. There was no way she should have fallen for Curt's sweet nothings and kind gestures. How in the world did she end up giving her body to him again?

God, forgive her, but it eased all her stress.

Chapter Twenty-Four

"You should probably go home so that things aren't suspicious, you know?" Curt asked her.

She shook her head in disagreement and stayed facing the wall of his bedroom. She was wrapped tightly in his sheets and both hands were tucked under her cheek. Guilt, anger, confusion, and sorrow filled her heart, and were reflected on her expression. She hated that she had been so weak just now. Curt, on the other hand, was beside her and lighting up a cigarette in satisfaction. Their lovemaking was probably a dream come true for him.

"What's the matter?" he questioned when he did not hear from her.

"Nothing. I can't go back. I don't want to live with him, knowing he's out doing all kinds of foolishness," she said and eventually unwrapped herself from the sheets and pulled each leg one by one out of the bed. "Thank you, though."

"For?"

"For taking my mind off of things for a little bit," she explained, as she got dressed.

"Where are you heading?" he called out to her and continued to suck on his mentholated Marlboro. She wondered why so many people smoked those things. They stunk and were unhealthy.

"Anywhere but home. I don't even know."

"Stay here then," he suggested and left the warmth of his bed. He approached her with his arms open. She accepted his hug. "It's no problem at all. You know I enjoy your company anyway."

"I don't know."

"Think about it," he said simply and kissed her. "I won't pressure you."

Clearly, he had a hold on her because even as she wished to leave, there was something that always kept Lorraina coming back. Perhaps it was the protection that he offered, or the companionship that she longed as she tried to figure out what life would be without Jhalil. It could also have been the sex that was amazing, but still not as good as Jhalil's. She missed him, but she refused to return home. She promised herself that she would ignore all phone calls and text messages from Jhalil.

"I'm only going back there to get my things. I left a box with some personal items in it," she told him and headed for the shower.

"Let me know if you need me." He retreated back to the bed, and she could hear his snores not long after.

As she showered and then dressed in the outfit from the day before, she could feel the guilt seeping into her heart. Despite all that was going on, she had cheated on Jhalil, plain and simple. Not only that, but she knew she was grieving the Holy Spirit because she had completely broken her vow to remain celibate until marriage. She had gone back to her old ways of fornicating, and it wasn't a good look. She had allowed her emotions to get the best of her.

She decided not to disturb Curt. It would make things worse if he trailed along, so she went back to her old home to grab her garments and a few forgotten necessities. Thankfully, his car wasn't in the driveway, so she had time to herself. Hurriedly, she walked through the house and stuffed the remaining items into the duffle bag she brought along. As she picked up the last of her makeup and personal hygiene items, she could hear a car door slam in the distance.

Her heart dropped. It could either be a neighbor, or it could be Jhalil. With her luck, she was certain it was her ex. Sure enough, as she looked out the bedroom window, she saw him exiting the car and admiring her car that was positioned in his spot. If she could, she would have slapped herself for taking so long. It had been exactly 22 minutes that she had been scavenging through the house. Now she would have to face him.

She swallowed the lump in her throat and prepared for the worse as she headed downstairs. By now, he was entering the house and calling her name. "Where are you, baby?"

Just the sound of his voice made her cringe.

"Don't call me that, and don't try to stop me. As a matter of fact, don't say *anything* to me," she warned as she approached him. "Let's just make this as seamless as possible."

"Why are you doing this? Your note said you knew everything," he explained and tried to reach out to touch her. "What exactly do you know? I'm sure it's far from the truth."

He looked good. *Darn* good. She had to look away.

"What did I say? Don't say anything to me. I have moved on, Jhalil, and you can call *this* off." She pulled off her engagement ring. It had not even made an indentation on her finger—that's how quickly it was on and off.

"Lorraina, please, let me explain."

"That's the problem. You should have said something a *loooong* time ago. Maybe I would have taken you back had I known something. It's too late now. Please get some help," she suggested and shrugged off his hands. She hoisted her bag onto her shoulder and left out with his painful pleas ringing in her ears.

As she pulled off, she saw him in the doorway with his hands on his head in distress. Tears streamed down his face, and she tried her best to ignore it in the rearview.

***

Weeks later, Lorraina was still at Curt's home, living rent-free, while she made strides to rebuild her life once again. She was just arriving home from a grocery trip, and the first thing that met her at the door was Curt holding up a wrapped box. He took her brown, paper bags from her and sat the box in her unexpected hands.

"Open up," he ordered and began to put the frozen foods in the freezer.

"A gift for *me?*" she asked with a smile.

"Mmhmm. Open up," he repeated.

Life was still strange for Lorraina. She had quickly fallen into the role of Curt's *unofficial* live-in girlfriend, and he loved it. She cooked, cleaned, and kept up the house like any good woman would, and he was glad that she had been broken down so easily. He thought that she would be uncomfortable with the entire idea of living together and starting over with him. He gave her an allowance to do what she needed to do, as his thanks to her. The gifts were plentiful, and they had made love at least three more times. She felt guilty for her shortcomings, but she had nowhere to turn to, and needed the hole in her heart filled.

Curt just happened to be that person.

Lorraina's fingers tore delicately at the wrapping paper until a white, rectangular box was revealed. She continued to smirk as she discarded the top of the box, pushed aside the glittery red tissue paper, and then was met with a folded garment. She eased the material out of the box and held it up to her body. It was a dress that was straight out of an expensive catalogue and was made with the gentlest of care. She could see herself in it, and she longed to feel the soft satin against her body. She wondered why Curt had gotten it for her. Not that she was ungrateful, but she was just curious.

Before she could ask, he pulled her body against his so they could peer into the full-length mirror together. He held her hips in place and began to kiss along her neck as she continued to admire the dress against her body.

"You like it?" he questioned in between kisses.

"I love it. but what's the occasion?"

"A work gathering. My boss is retiring after 52 years of service. I want you to be my date tonight."

"*Tonight*? Oh, wow," she whispered and slowly placed the dress back into the box.

He noticed her uninterested response and change in attitude. "What's wrong?"

"I don't know, Curt." She slid her fingers across the box unsurely.

"What do you mean? You don't want to go with me?"

"Maybe we should slow this down— whatever it is that we have. I don't think I should go for the simple fact that we're not a couple. We're not together," she explained harshly. "We're just sort of going through the motions, but…"

"What do you call this then?" He motioned around the room and gave her an incredulous look. "Your clothes and personal items are everywhere at *my* house. You're cooking and cleaning at *my* house. We're sexing on every inch of the room, and you're saying we're not together? Oh, okay. I'm not sure what world YOU live in, but that means something to me."

"Curt…"

"You know what? Whatever, Lorraina. I'm glad I kept the receipt. I'll take the dress back and go by myself." He huffed and snatched the box from her hands.

She stared at his back in shock. "So that's what you want to do? You want to storm off like you're crazy? And you think I want to be in a relationship with someone like *that*? What happened to talking things out?"

"I'm tired of talking things out! I just want to be with you. You're so stubborn that you can't see that."

"We're living in sin, for one. Just last month, I was with another man. Correction: I was ENGAGED to him and on the path to becoming the first lady of OUR church! That doesn't even sound right in *my* ears," she screamed. "I'm all screwed up right now, and my life has changed forever with the information you gave me, so don't fault me if I just want to take things slow. I can't afford to go through any more surprises, setbacks, or heartbreaks. I would hope that you could understand that."

"But an office party? You act like I asked you to marry me!" he yelled and then caught himself. He exhaled and calmed down some. "It's just an innocent function. I'm not asking for anything but my friend to come with me and enjoy dinner, dancing, and socializing with a bunch of old, white people," he joked.

Lorraina laughed as well and then reluctantly took his face in her hands. She did not kiss him, but spoke against his lips, "I would love to escort you to the party...*friend*."

They ate a light lunch, and then showered in separate bathrooms to prepare for the night.

Lorraina was a natural beauty, and her gorgeous features did not necessarily need any enhancement, but she still loved a little mascara, eyeliner, and bold lip color. She wore her dark hair down and it seemed to flow with ease since it was freshly washed. She wore a diamond choker, and a pair of diamond teardrop earrings. The ocean blue dress was zipped up her petite back and it touched mid-thigh on her. With every stride, her toned legs could be seen. She chose shoes that had a chunky heel and showed off her shimmery nail polish. Curt mentioned dancing and she did not want to tire her feet out.

As she rounded the corner, Curt stood in the middle of the floor, buttoning his shirt. He paused and eyed her from her toes to the top of her head in awe. "You look amazing," he complimented.

"Thank you," she said with a blush. "It's a perfect fit. How did you know my size?"

"I've studied your body every time it stood before me naked. I know you have beautiful wide hips and plump thighs. I also know you have larger breasts, and a perfectly round butt. When I saw the dress, it just called out to me; I knew it would frame your body in all the right places," he spoke passionately and shrugged as if it were no big deal.

For a second time, she blushed and remained quiet. Although she did not love him, she knew it was a reason that she stuck around. He was a charmer, and he knew how to treat and talk to a woman. It would be fun seeing where this road took them, but for the time being, she appreciated his kindness and compliments.

Contrary to what Curt had told her, the room was filled with middle-aged men and women dressed skimpily. It was a diverse crowd of blacks, whites, and everyone in between. When they entered the hall, most of the individuals were kissing, hugging intimately, or just flat-out having sex. Lorraina paused as she walked in and looked at him.

"What did we just walk into?"

"I told you. It's my lieutenant's retirement party. I guess he wanted to go out with a...*bang*," Curt joked as he pointed to an older gentleman in the corner of the room who had two women on either side of him as he was fed grapes.

Lorraina must have stepped into some horrible 70s porno. There was no way she was going to stick around to see what happened next at this giant orgy. She felt uncomfortable and the room had an unpleasant scent already. She shook her head and turned towards the door.

"I don't want to be here. Are you kidding me?"

"Oh, come on. We can just stay a half-hour and then be on our way. You're here with me. I won't let anybody do anything to you," he promised.

Lorraina still looked around unsurely, but she followed behind him and tried to make herself feel more comfortable. They settled at an empty table and there was a bottle of wine waiting for them.

"No, thank you," she said before he could reach for the corkscrew. "I don't drink."

"But you do everything else under the sun? Oh, okay," Curt said with a laugh. He poured himself a glass and downed it. "You sure you don't want any?"

"I'm positive." Lorraina looked around and was still in shock at what was going on around them. She felt out of place and…overdressed. She joked, "Is this what you guys normally do at the office?"

"It's a party 'round here every day," he chuckled mischievously.

"Y'all are some kinky folks apparently," she mumbled half-heartedly.

Lorraina and Curt were the talk of the town. Everybody's eyes seemed to migrate towards them, and then finally, a woman walked up to them as they finished their finger foods.

"Oh, my goodness. You must be Lorraina. Curt talks about you often." The woman rubbed her upper back.

"He *does*?" Lorraina raised her eyebrows at him.

"Yes, even though I knew about you before he even mentioned your name." The woman winked. "You're that pastor who had that sex scandal going on a little while back. I watched your video that went viral. You're impressive…just stunning."

She was referring to the sex tape that had been leaked by the conniving deacon at her old church.

Lorraina shuddered and realized right then that she could never truly run from her past. The woman looked at her with lust in her eyes and no inch of Lorraina's body went unnoticed. She squirmed with discomfort and looked to Curt for help, but he seemed to be enjoying this. Was this woman hitting on her? Lorraina had to get out of there.

"I think it's time to go. I'm tired, and it's been more than 30 minutes," she reminded him as she gathered her purse and began to stand.

"Leaving so soon?" the woman questioned and leaned closer to Lorraina. The woman's hand landed on Lorraina's hip. "I haven't really gotten a chance to know you yet."

"And honey, with breath that bad, you never will. Excuse me. *Move* back," Lorraina ordered and pushed past the woman.

She could swear that she heard the woman call her out of her name, but she did not care. She had made a mistake even coming here. She had made a mistake trusting Curt to do the right thing. Obviously, his mind and intentions were somewhere else.

"Let's go *now*, Curt," she commanded.

She walked briskly towards the exit, but Curt was much quicker and stronger as he yanked her back into his body. He whispered menacingly, "Did you have to be so rude? That was one of my long-time partners."

"Okay, and? You said you would protect me from these heathens. That woman was flirting with me. She crossed the line first."

"It's harmless. Calm down."

"I want to go home! NOW!"

He wrapped his hand tighter around her arm and then turned her to face him. "Close your eyes."

"Take me home," she demanded. "I'm serious, Curt. This is not my crowd. I don't know why you even brought me here. This isn't really a retirement party, is it?"

"Close…your…eyes," he repeated and gave her a stern look. He never answered her question either.

She looked around and saw that people were staring. She reluctantly did as told and breathed out a sigh. Curt placed his hand on each side of her face, and then kissed her passionately. She could feel his tongue intertwine with hers. She also felt something grainy and flavorless that was transferred from his mouth to hers. She opened her eyes and attempted to protest, not knowing what he had done, but he held her in place.

"Stop," she mumbled against his lips and struggled to free herself. "What is that?"

Curt would not ease up. Finally, when she could sense that the tasteless mint or whatever candy that was in her mouth had dissolved, Curt released his hold on her. She slapped him with all her strength and backed away from him. He looked shocked that she had hit him and charged towards her. He grabbed her arm so tightly that she was certain there would be a bruise there later.

"Why would you do that?" he questioned her.

"Why would you do *that*? You know what? This was all a mistake. Take me home!" she cried and wiped her mouth. She could feel her mouth producing extra saliva suddenly. "What was that in your mouth?"

All eyes were on them while he practically drug her to sit down. "Lower your voice!"

"Take me home!" she screamed. "Or I'll call a cab. Either way, I'm done with you."

"Weren't you always done with me? You were always stuck on stupid and stuck on Jhalil. But I told you *I* get the last laugh," he warned and waved his hand to a group of men who had been watching them all night. "You're going to wish you never played with me."

Lorraina did not understand a word he was saying. She swallowed hard as she watched the men, one by one, toss a few bills on the table for the waitstaff and then made their way over. An uneasy feeling formed at the pit of her stomach. Curt was nothing but trouble and this night was confirming it more and more for her. She began to silently pray.

"Curt, my man. What's going on?" the front man of the group spoke and then nodded towards Lorraina. "Good evening, beautiful. Glad you could join us; Curt has told us so much about you."

That seemed to be the reoccurring theme. To be so new, their "relationship" sure was on everybody's minds. Lorraina kept quiet. She had no words. Besides, she was beginning to feel a little dizzy and disoriented. She could not understand what was causing her sudden illness, because she had only eaten chicken wings, cheese cubes, and a few celery sticks. She placed her hand on her stomach.

"You're just as gorgeous as he described," another man chimed in and rubbed the hair along his jawline. "Are you ready to entertain us?"

Lorraina's eyes squinted, and she cocked her head to the side. Her equilibrium was all off at this point. "Entertain *who*? Me?"

"Isn't that why you brought her?" He looked over to Curt who nodded.

Lorraina felt nauseous but managed to keep it down as she put her hands up. Her eyes were watering, and she could feel her stomach rumbling with queasiness. "I'm not doing anything for anybody. I'm ready to go home…NOW!"

"Give me a second, y'all," Curt said while he reached for his phone. He checked the battery, saw that it was still high, and then tossed it to one of the men. "Hook it up and play some music she can dance to."

"Who's dancing?" Lorraina asked lowly. "I'm not…I'm not d…" Her mouth felt flimsy, as if she could not form any words.

Curt chuckled and pulled her onto his lap. He kissed along the side of her face as she began to heave. "You good, baby?"

"I—I don't feel so well," she moaned. "Pl— please take me home."

"I will. Just give us one dance."

"Noooo," she whimpered and attempted to hold her head up, but it kept falling limp back onto Curt's shoulder.

He stood up and brought her along with him to the center of the room. By now, the dance floor had been cleared, and all eyes were on them as some people cheered and other people whipped out their cameras. Lorraina, unable to really verbalize any more words, was unsure what was taking place as she stumbled behind Curt.

"Ladies and gentlemen," Curt announced in a microphone. "It would be my pleasure to introduce you to my beautiful friend, Lorraina. I wanted nothing more than to be her man, but she's rejected me time and time again. Oh, that rhymed."

The crowd "awwwed."

"No worries. She told me she would make it up to me now by giving you all a little entertainment. There's nothing crazier than a swingers' party, am I right?"

The people hooted and hollered in agreement.

Swingers' party? Lorraina thought. *He said it was his boss's retirement party.*

Even in her state, she realized that Curt had lied to her and brought her out here to make a fool of her. She realized he had lied to her up until this point and had gone on a sick venture for revenge. He had worked hard to mislead, manipulate, and hurt her for what she had done to him so many moons ago. She tried to drag her heavy feet off the dance floor, but it felt like each leg weighed a ton. Curt caught her as she tried to run but stumbled.

"Ah, ah, ah. Where are you going? *Dance.* Otherwise, I'm going to take you in the back and let Roman and Ishmael do whatever they want to you."

She followed his eyes to where two men were off to the side, staring at her hungrily. Lorraina was stuck in a room full of impure, promiscuous people that had not a moral or care in the world. She looked around helplessly as music began to play and she was ordered to dance. She felt dirty and unclean, and ignored the looks of men and women from all over as they stared holes through her clothing. She lost her balance as Curt proceeded to rip her dress apart and do everything he promised not to. She finally blacked out when several men surrounded her and led her to the back of the building.

Chapter Twenty-Five

"How does that feel, love?"

The question came as Lorraina's calves were being massaged, and she could honestly say that she needed it. She could not remember ever feeling so relaxed and tended to. The room was dark with a single candle lit, and her body was stretched across some smooth surface. She had no idea how she ended up clothed in a robe and fuzzy socks, but she did not care. The warm hands caressing her legs made it all better.

"It feels good," she whispered back.

"You've been so stressed. I wanted to ease your mind."

That voice. She quivered at the sound of that voice.

"I was thinking we should talk," he continued.

The more he spoke, the less she realized it was not Curt.

"Talk about what?" she asked while she turned to look over her shoulder.

"Let's talk about these lies they're putting on my name."

Lorraina turned completely and to her surprise, Jhalil was facing her with tears rolling down his face. She pushed away from him in disgust, but he was much too strong. He held her legs in place while he pleaded for her to stop running from him.

"Get off me! You're SICK!" she screamed and scrambled to regain her footing, but Jhalil continued to hold her down.

"Listen to me! Everything he's told you is a lie! He's just trying to separate us."

"WHO?"

"You KNOW who! Just think about it! Please believe me!" Jhalil pleaded again.

She searched the depths of his eyes to see if he was serious. There was nothing but truth permeating his brown eyes. She reached out to cup her hands around his face, but in an instant, he was gone.

Lorraina jumped awake in a cold sweat.

"Jhalil? Come back!" she cried out and then slapped a hand over her mouth.

Her shoulders shook in fear and her gown and hair was drenched with sweat. She felt like she had been in a sauna. Her heart thumped erratically in her chest as she tried to interpret her previous dream. All she wanted was to talk to Jhalil now. Perhaps they had all been wrong about him.

"Jesus! What is wrong with me?" she asked aloud.

Tears flowed from her saddened eyes as she looked around the dark room and tried to comprehend where she was. Then it hit her. For the last week, she had been cooped up in the hospital. That night of the party, she had been drugged and according to the nurses assigned to her room, she had been manhandled, violated, and all but raped.

The swingers party attack, which had been orchestrated by Curt, was broadcasted on Facebook Live, and had gone viral up until the video was reported and taken down. For the second time, Lorraina's body had been put out on the Internet for all to see. For the second time, Lorraina's integrity, reputation, and self-esteem had been torn down and degraded. Family, friends, and old cohorts all reached out to her at the hospital to see if she was okay, including her former bishop.

For two entire days, she had been in a coma because of the effects of the roofies that Curt had slipped in her drink and in her mouth that night. Doctors told her that it was a wonder she had survived the doses—it had to be God. But sadly, because of the ordeal, Noah had since then been handed over to local authorities to find him a forever home. It was not what she wanted, but it was court ordered and she had no say so in the matter.

It was obvious Curt really cared about her before that night's incident. The only problem was his care was obsessive and she learned that when he loved, he loved hard. He had become obsessed with loving her and loving *on* her. She realized that he was sick; he had a problem with rejection, and he was still punishing her for things he could not control.

He made it a mission to get her back for when he and Jhalil fought. He told her often that he would get the last laugh, and she assumed this is what he was talking about. He had played a game and she was his pawn, so he got what he wanted. Lorraina was stripped of everything and had to face the consequences of playing with his heart. She could hang up the idea of rebuilding her reputation; it seemed she would be known as "the promiscuous pastor" for as long as she lived.

During this downtime, she thought of Jhalil heavily. She thought about what Curt had revealed to her and wondered if he ever told the truth. She wondered if he had made up everything just to separate them and keep them apart. Whatever the case, she missed Jhalil dearly and could not stop thinking about his love and the beautiful history that they built. Her strange dream grabbed her attention as well. She was so confused and needed answers...the *right* answers from the *right* source.

"God, wherever he is right now, please give him peace and may the truth set *him* free," she said, ending her prayer for Jhalil.

She searched for her phone throughout the mangled blankets, and then finally found the device. She sent a message after much hesitation and knew he would not respond to her, especially with her leaving him abruptly. He was probably snoring up under another woman and she could not be mad at him. She didn't want his life to stop because of her foolishness. Regardless, she just needed to hear from *him*.

Her heartstrings were being pulled because she had not given him a chance. She had not allowed him to explain anything to her. As much as she loved him, she had shut him completely out. Not only that, but she had also run into Curt's arms and never looked back. That was unfair to Jhalil and she regretted her decisions now. Hopefully, they would get the opportunity to talk things out, if only for the sake of closure.

As she rolled over and got into a more comfortable position, her phone buzzed. It was Jhalil, writing her back. Actually, he was calling her back. She sighed with anticipation, looked towards the door that was still closed, and then answered the phone.

"Yes?"

"Lorraina?"

"It's me. Hey."

"Baby!" Her insides tingled at the pet name. Maybe he wasn't too angry or upset with her. "Oh, my God! What happened to you? Where did you go? Why did you leave?"

"Jhalil, we need to talk."

"Obviously! What made you run off? Just answer me that."

Lorraina closed her eyes. "Curt, and before you say anything, tell me. Is it true?"

"Is *what* true?" he repeated and when she was reluctant to answer, he questioned her again. "Is what true, Rain? Just say it. We don't need any more miscommunication or misunderstandings."

She rolled her eyes up to the ceiling, trying to word everything correctly. "Are you a pimp, and have you been participating in the exploitation of women and children?"

"What? Are you for real right now?" His voice grew loud and shaky with bewilderment. "God, NO! What would make you say that? Of course, I'm not a pimp and I'm not exploiting anybody."

Lorraina's eyes closed. "Who are all those women then, Jay? Why do you have so many identification cards and aliases? I ran into some women in a bathroom, and they said you had a briefcase of money, offering it to them. I—I even saw you out that one day with another woman having dinner downtown. Who were they, and why were you with them? Answer me!"

"Wait. Slow down! Slow down. That's why we need to talk. Of all things, why would you think I could be that lowdown and dirty? That's a coward's move! You know I could never abuse or hurt anybody, especially women or children. Those women were prostitutes that…"

"Oh, so you're *admitting* that you were cheating though?" she interrupted.

"LISTEN, Lorraina. You have to listen to me. You said you want the truth, and I should have given it to you long ago. I was going to pay those ladies in order to get them off the streets."

"Oh, yeah?" She rolled her eyes.

"I swear to you! It's the same thing with that young lady at the restaurant downtown. Saving women from sex trafficking has been a mission of mine for a while now. I see these cats out here plotting and trying to blindside these women, and I've tried to be an advocate for those victims for some years now. I just never knew how to come out and tell you," he explained.

"So, Jhalil..."

"I'm not done, baby. This must be said. Please listen. When I started doing this, it sounded CRAZY. It made no sense to anybody, and only a couple people know about and support what I do. I should've told you sooner, and for that, I apologize because it does seem bad on the outside looking in."

She swallowed hard with impending regret.

"You're the woman I want to marry, and I've been saying that since I met you," Jhalil continued. "It was a secret that was eating me alive, but I didn't want to hurt you in any way, and look. I still ended up hurting you. Baby, you have to believe me!"

"Oh, my God," she spoke softly with remorse. "Oh, my God. I believe you. I should have always believed you. What did I do?"

"Shhh. I know, I know. God led me to complete this assignment—myself and another good friend of mine—and to date, we've helped more than 32 women and children."

Her heart broke all over again. This man was doing the Lord's work, while she had been over some other man's house and plotting on his downfall. She felt awful as she rubbed her hand over her forehead and tried to calm her racing heart.

"That is phenomenal. I—I can't apologize enough."

"Where are you?" he pondered. "Can I see you now? I'll pick you up."

"Yes," she answered without reluctance and then looked down at her hospital garments and the IV sticking in her arm. "Wait, *no.*"

"Well, where are you? Is Noah nearby you? I've missed you both so much. God, I wish I could've gotten this all squared away before this happened."

Lorraina felt two inches tall now. How was she going to explain everything that had taken place? It was like a movie that was playing out before her eyes, and she was the star of it. Honestly, she was shocked that he hadn't seen her in the circulating video, so she knew he was clueless as to *what* she had been up to.

She had to make this right no matter how she figured that this was not going to end well for her. No matter how much she planned and prayed, God Himself was going to have to step in and work everything out for her.

"Give me a day or two to come back. I promise I will. I just need…"

"Time?" He completed her sentence. "I understand, baby. Take whatever time you need. I know it's late, and I know it's still hard for you. But please come back to me. I haven't been able to eat, sleep, or minister properly without you."

"I promise."

"Goodnight, baby. I'll talk to you soon, okay? I love you."

"Yeah. I—I love you too."

She nodded as if he could see her and then ended the phone call. No sooner than she tucked her phone under her pillow and began to weep did a knock sound at her door. It was Curt, who should have been locked up and rotting slowly in somebody's prison. She attempted to reach for the button that would alert the nurse, but by then, he was standing before her and yanking her arm down. He went back to lock the doors and then walked to the bed.

"You're awake."

"Yeah."

"Everything all right?"

"No. Not at all," Lorraina admitted. "And you know why everything's not alright."

She decided not to reveal to Curt that she had talked with Jhalil. She wanted to play dumb for the moment. After all, he was dangerous, and he was the one who had given her the false information. His motives this entire time had been to get closer to her, and like an idiot, she had fallen for his lies. Come to think of it, she had never seen a badge, squad car, uniform, or federal agent's ID. She had not been to his workplace, nor did she really believe that Curt was really who he said he was anymore.

All she had done was follow her emotions, and it had gotten her in deep trouble. She had been fooled and then assaulted by strangers and had nearly lost the love of her life in the process. None of this had been worth it.

"What's the matter?" He saw the look on her face and furrowed his eyebrows.

Her innocent act could not be contained any longer as she spoke angrily, "You need to leave immediately. Are you kidding me? Why are you here like everything's okay?"

"What do you mean?" Curt sat on the edge of the bed and rubbed her leg. "Would you like a foot rub?"

"Don't touch me! You're a liar, and you put me in harm's way!" she yelled and attempted to reach for her cell phone on the food tray. "Curt, how long have you been a federal agent? Where's your office located?"

He cocked his head. "What's with all of the questions? I told you what I did for a living."

"No, Emilio and Julio did. I have no idea who they are or who they're working for. What was the purpose of lying on Jhalil?"

"What are you talking about?" He kept an unreadable expression on his face. "Are you serious right now? You think I lied to you?"

"I'm not saying anything. I just want to know where your proof for all of this is?"

Curt gritted his teeth. "So, you still love him. Is that what it is?"

"I'll always love him," she vowed and looked him in the eye. "Now, tell me the truth."

He stood up and snatched the covers from the bed angrily. Then he took her by the arm and threw her down. She tumbled onto the floor and winced in pain while he ranted, "After all I've done for you. I've given you a place to stay. I gave you money! I've cooked MEALS for you. I've run up my credit, buying nice things for YOU. This is the thanks I get? I loved you!"

"Curt, cut the act," she screamed from the floor, hoping someone came to her rescue. "You left me out there to be touched and violated by sick, perverted men! You put me out there on the Internet where people laughed at me, mocked me, and called me all kinds of names. You lied to me so that I could leave Jhalil. That's not love. You caused all of this!"

"*I* did that? Nah, you sleepin' around and playin' with people's emotions did that!"

"I didn't play with your emotions. I don't know what to think anymore about you. I tried to give you the benefit of the doubt, and all you've done is continue to harass and hurt me. Do I owe you something? Just tell me that. What do you want from me exactly?"

He knelt beside her and looked at her with disgust. "After all that body's been through, and after all the men that have touched you, I'm a fool to think that I was worthy of it."

"Don't you dare talk down on me now that I've figured out this game you're playing. You weren't worried about how many men I've been with when you were sleeping with me! Why do you hate me and Jhalil's relationship so much?"

"Because he can't love you like I can!" he yelled, and his voice seemed to shake the walls. "Just wait! You haven't seen the last of me, Lorraina. Go home to your man and enjoy him while he's still free."

Okay, he was truly delusional, but she also knew his threats might be serious. As he stormed out of the room, she yanked the IV out of her arm, and gathered her belongings. She did not even care to get fully dressed and ignored the nurse's pleas for her to take it easy.

She caught an Uber to her old home and hoped to God that Jhalil was still awake, and she could explain everything to him. Time went by quickly, and before long, she sat outside of what was once their home. She banged on the front door and leaned against it. She could almost smell his cologne seconds before he opened the door. Lorraina jumped into his unexpected arms and cradled her face in his neck.

"I'm so sorry, baby! Please forgive me," she pleaded.

"Shhh. What matters now is that you're back here with me." He did not realize she had on a hospital gown; that's how emotional he was as he cradled her in his arms.

They both cried as he maneuvered their bodies away from the door and upstairs.

"What happened to us?" he asked softly. "Don't ever leave me again."

"I won't. I promise," she vowed.

He looked down at her body in curiosity. "Why do you have this on? What happened to you? Did Curt hurt you?" There was anger in his eyes and timbre in his voice.

She almost wanted to smile because she could feel the love permeating his body. He still loved her, and he cared about her well-being.

"Let's just talk in the morning," she suggested and kissed his cheek. "I need a bath and sleep. We can get everything out in the open another day."

But that conversation never happened. It was in the wee hours of the following morning that they were each jolted from peaceful slumber. Lorraina lifted her head from Jhalil's chest where they had fallen asleep on the day bed. She could hear two knocks and then a loud *bang*.

Before long, voices and footsteps rushed in like an army. It was like they were in a movie scene, where police raided a drug lord's home and searched for weapons and narcotics. She held the blanket up to her body as she watched police officers storm into the room and command to know where Jhalil Harrison was.

He held up his hands, told them his name calmly, and then was tackled to the ground. Lorraina cried out as police officers arrested the man she was madly in love with, and eventually taken forcefully down to a police car where he was told his rights.

Lorraina searched the men's faces, searched their uniforms for badges or identification numbers, but saw none. She found that strange.

"Why am I being arrested?" he questioned for the umpteenth time.

Finally, the black police officer turned to him and replied, "You're being arrested for the assault, verbal abuse, and threats that you made towards Mr. Curtis Randall. Watch your head."

Lorraina stumbled against the concrete in shock and watched as Jhalil was shoved into the vehicle.

"Lorraina, call my lawyer! Don't say anything to anyone about this. I'll be okay, baby. I'll see you soon," Jhalil promised.

Even he seemed unsure of his fate.

Their eyes locked through the window, and she shed a tear for him. Red, blue, and clear lights flashed but no sirens rang out into the night. Instead, the car pulled off and disappeared down the road within seconds. A few of the neighbors rushed out to see what had taken place, but she ignored their questions and ran back into the house. The fingers could only point to one vengeful person again—*Curt.*

Chapter Twenty-Six

There was no way that this was happening. There was no way that Jhalil had just been arrested. Lorraina rushed to get dressed, and then searched his office until she came across his lawyer's name and number. She explained the situation to the attorney, tucked a wad of money in her purse, and then headed for her car so that she could go to the local precinct.

A dark car waited outside of their home now, and she knew who it was before he even left the confinements of his car.

"Why are you playing games? What do you want from US?" she screamed. "Him being arrested is what you wanted all along, isn't it?"

Curt leaned against the car and crossed his arms. "I told you I was going to have the last laugh in this, right?"

"You are crazy, you know that? I hate you!" she screamed with infuriation.

"No. *You're* the crazy one." He smiled widely. "You slept with me first, then you met Jhalil, slept with him and got engaged, then you left him and slept with me *again*, and then you went crawlin' back to your man. That's not a good look, Lorraina. Have a little respect for yourself."

She spoke through gritted teeth, "Why would you trick me like that? You knew what you were doing all along and then you made Jhalil out to be this monster."

"You're right. I *did* know what I was doing. Jhalil told me all about his mission when we first met and told me how nervous he was to tell you. I used what I already knew and played along with it to my advantage, and most importantly, I got what I wanted out the deal. *Sue* me."

Lorraina lunged for him, but he dodged her arms and held her in place. The strength of his arms overpowered her, so her struggle was no match for him. He looked unbothered and unimpressed with the way that she was fighting against him as he slammed her into his car door.

"Are you done?" he questioned.

"How could you do this to me?"

"Get over yourself, Lorraina. You can't go around screwing people over and then the second someone does something to you, you want to act like a victim. It doesn't work like that."

Lorraina spat in his face. It was a lowdown move and she was surprised at her own boldness, but she could not help herself. Curtis jumped back in surprise and released his hold on her in the process. He shook his head in disgust and wiped a hand across his face. No sooner than when his vision was clear did he take the back of his hand and slam it into the side of her face. She fell because of the forcefulness.

"Leave me alone!" she screamed. "Don't...don't touch me or say anything else to me!"

He mumbled a few words in frustration that she could not understand and then reached into his back pocket. He slammed a box down into her lap and turned to walk away. It was a ring box.

"To think that I was going to propose to you," he whispered.

"I don't *love* you, Curtis, nor do I want to be with you. Why can't you understand that? Jhalil has my heart. A proposal would not have changed anything."

He said nothing more and then settled in his car.

She could not understand why he would even waste his time. It was not like they were head over heels in love. They had slept around a few times, went on a few mediocre dates, and engaged in casual conversation; there was nothing more to their story. He had comforted her while she was going through, but ultimately, it was his lies that had pushed her into his arms.

Perhaps there was truly something off in his mind to make him do these things. Whatever the case was, she could not understand why she continued to find herself in the wrong situations with so many men, from Capri to Curtis and Deacon Donnell and even with Jhalil.

She remained planted on the ground even as he zoomed off down the road. She tossed the ring somewhere in the bushes and reluctantly picked herself up from the ground.

She had to get to the bottom of this and free her man.

Lorraina's first stop was attempting to follow the police car that had taken Jhalil away. She Googled the nearest precinct, jumped in her car and took off down the lonesome road, searching for the police car. It had not been more than 10 minutes since they left, yet there was no spotting of any squad car. Even as she squinted and looked far ahead, she could see no indication of a law enforcement vehicle. She was confused.

This road was the only one that people could take until they reached the main street, so she was confused by its emptiness. Her neck careened around the area, and she caught movement out of the corner of her eye. Her first thought was a deer hiding in the bushes, so she swerved and stayed close to the side of the road.

But no deer ever appeared. She rolled down her window and swallowed hard. "Who's out there?"

When she heard a slight rustling, she thought of the *Lifetime* movies where people stuck around and got murdered, so she sped off and did not look back. She headed to the precinct that she had Googled. In fact, it was the *only* precinct for miles, so she knew Jhalil had to have been booked here. She was surprised when everybody looked at her like she was crazy.

"You said your boyfriend was arrested? Ma'am, this town is as slow as a tortoise. We haven't had any arrests or disturbances since early last week."

Lorraina shook her head and stared at the man who had a southern drawl. "What do you mean? You guys JUST left my house."

"Impossible. We're short staffed today, and the few who are here have been sitting around talking for the last few hours. No one has left this building and I would know…I'm the executive secretary," he said proudly.

Lorraina smiled sarcastically. "Good for you. Seriously, I need to clear my fiancé of whatever charges he may have. It was all a big misunderstanding."

"Ma'am…if it'll ease your concerns, would you like to take a look at our booking area? There is no one here."

Lorraina followed him around the building and sure enough, there was not a single criminal or regular civilian in sight. This police station was literally waiting for something—*anything*—to happen. Lorraina, though she was confused and growing agitated, could not help wondering how boring that must be for all of them to have nothing better to do.

"Thank you for your help," she said dejectedly and walked away.

As she headed to her car, she could hear them laughing through the open windows at her foolishness. They thought she was either on drugs and hallucinating, or just carrying out a joke too long. She settled in her car and hit her hands against the steering wheel in frustration.

"What do I do? God, what do I do? Where could you be, Jay?" she asked no one in particular. This was killing her.

She suddenly got the urge to head back home so she drove a little bit above the speed limit and headed to their house. This time, as she drove through the well-manicured trees surrounding the driveway, she slowed down and eyed the area where she had heard movement earlier. Her eyes caught a trail of blood leading further up the road, so she followed it and prayed the entire time.

There was either an animal hurt, or it was whom she feared was hurt.

"Jhalil. Oh, my God," she whispered and finally saw him crawling in the opposite direction.

She parked and rushed out of the car and called out to him. His shoulders were slumped, and his head was lowered. He crawled at a slow pace and fell every so often. His knees and the palms of his hands were bloodied. His nose looked disfigured, as if it had been broken under the force of someone's fists. There was a deep cut above his eyebrow and purple and blue bruising had already claimed his once flawless skin. He breathed shallowly.

"Who did this to you?" she cried and dropped down beside him. The question was rhetorical, but he shook his head and tried to verbalize an answer. "Shhh. Save your breath. Hang on, baby."

She could just cry right then and there, but she held it together so that she could call for help. The dispatcher on the other end promised that an ambulance would be over shortly. In the meantime, she took off her windbreaker, and wrapped him tightly in it. She rocked his body back and forth and stayed on the ground with him while her headlights blared in their faces. It grew colder and rain began to fall just as she caught the faint sirens of an ambulance.

"Help is on the way, baby. Help is on the way."

Chapter Twenty-Seven

Jhalil's mind raced a mile a minute as Lorraina sobbed and held him in her arms. Even with so much pain and discomfort, he could not help but think if this was all part of some sick plan she had carried out to make him suffer. He knew everything; Curt had run it down to him detail by detail in the short ride in the unmarked police car. He thought back to what had just taken place and could not seem to wrap his mind around any of it.

"You understand why you're in this car?"

"I'm not saying anything else until my lawyer is present," Jhalil said and continued to look out the window.

"Naw, naw. I think you misunderstood my question," another voice entered the conversation.

Jhalil's eyes widened as he looked at the hooded individual in the passenger seat that he hadn't noticed before. It was Curt and he wore a smug grin on his face. It was then that he realized this entire thing was a setup. Jhalil rolled his eyes and knew he had just entered some mess. This man was still butt-hurt about him being with Lorraina and obviously couldn't handle rejection well.

"Long time, no see, my man," Curt spoke lowly.

"Let me out of this car. Let me out of these cuffs."

"I'll do so when I'm done," Curt said just as the car slowed to a stop. They had not covered much distance from the house. In fact, if Jhalil was able to turn around in the cuffs, he could still see the lights from his house in the near distance. Curt handed the driver a set of keys and then ordered, "Jerome, go pull my car up from down the street."

Jhalil eyed Curt as he exited the car and then came to his door. He opened it and Jhalil fell out slightly. He struggled to pull him up, and then finally was able to prop him up against the car.

"What is this? What kind of operation are you running?""

Curt punched him in his stomach and then shook his balled fist. "I'm the one that's going to be doing all the talking, you hear? Unless I ask you a question, keep your mouth closed."

Jhalil coughed and attempted to stand back up. The second he was able to compose himself, Curt punched him again in the same spot, and then kneed him in the groin. Jhalil fell to the ground this time and groaned.

Curt chuckled. "What's wrong? You can't take a punch?"

"Get these handcuffs off me and I'll show you what I can do," he said in between groans. "I did it before and you better hope I don't get the opportunity to lay you out again."

"Wah, wah, wah," Curt mocked and kneeled beside him. He held something in his hands. It was rectangular and black. Jhalil kept his eye on it until he was sure what it was. "Listen up. I'm going to make this short because I know your little whore will be on her way soon to find you."

Curt adjusted the object in his hand. It looked to be a recording device of some sort, because with a few presses of the red buttons, he could hear Lorraina and Curt's voices. It was clear as day that they were breathy and in proximity of one another. There was also the sound of lips touching skin, occasional moans, and the delicate thump of a headboard slamming against a wall. Finally, Lorraina cried out on the recording and told him that she had had enough, and the creak of mattress springs could be heard as the recording faded.

Jhalil wished he could block out the audio, but it was impossible. Curt held him down with his knee in his side, and began to play another portion of the recording.

"You promise to protect me?" Lorraina asked.

"I'll do anything you want me to do."

228

"What if Jhalil comes back and wants revenge? I'll help you take him down, but I need to know I'm safe when all this is said and done."

"I got you. I'll handle him. I'll make it so he disappears if you want me to."

"No, no. Don't do that. Don't kill him. Just teach him a lesson. Someone I trusted abused me as a child so my tolerance for this is nonexistent. Pedophiles of any kind deserve to be beaten and tortured."

"You want my guys to do that to him?"

"Do whatever you want. I don't care. But don't kill him. I just want to be done with…"

The recording stopped. Jhalil's eyes were glazed in shock as the recorded conversation registered in his mind. Curt kept quiet as he tucked the recorder in his pocket and then stood to his full height.

"I'm only doing what she asked," he said before slamming the heel of his foot into Jhalil's back and side.

Curt kicked him in the face, nearly breaking his nose. He proceeded to beat him up a few more minutes, before dragging his body into the shrubbery, and then unlocking the cuffs from around his wrists. Jhalil watched helplessly as Jerome pulled up in Curt's sports car, and he hopped back into the unmarked police car. Curt, instead of following Jerome, headed back to Jhalil's house.

Although he was shocked by Lorraina's harsh words, he prayed to God that Curt didn't hurt her as he drifted in and out of the darkness calling him. He finally came to when he heard a car slow down near where he was slumped over.

Assuming it was Curt coming back for more, he crawled as quickly as he could on a possibly shattered tibia, and throbbing, sliced hands where Curt had cruelly run his pocketknife across each of his palms. But it wasn't Curt; it was not Jerome, or any other fake police officer returning. It was the woman he had grown to love and hate and the woman who had gotten him in all this mess.

"Who did this to you?"

He could hear Lorraina cry out, as he finally breathed in relief. With her, even as conniving as she had been, he trusted that he would no longer have to fight for his life. He succumbed to the darkness and was out cold.

***

"Mr. Harrison?"

Jhalil stirred awake just as he felt a set of cool, gloved hands probe at his stomach. He winced and moaned for the woman to stop.

"I'm sorry. I just want to make sure there are no blood clots," the nurse assured him.

"What happened to me?" he whispered.

His throat was thick with swelling, and his voice was hoarse. His breath smelled horrid. He eyed the young woman who was probably no older than 22 or 23 and fresh out of college. She had rich, brown skin and the kinkiest, most beautiful hair he had ever seen that was flowing past her shoulders. She was petite with dimples for days and wore distinctive purple nail polish.

"Mr. Harrison, you favor Michael Ealy," she said as she began to peel away the soiled gauze that had been on his abdomen.

He winced in agony. "I've been told that before. Now can you tell me what happened to me?"

She looked unsure as she spoke, "Your injuries are not life-threatening, thankfully. Your surgery went well for your broken ribs."

"Broken ribs?"

She nodded and brushed a tendril of hair out of her face. "The doctor put in titanium plates to stabilize your ribs. You don't remember anything?"

"Vaguely," he groaned as he attempted to survey the damage on his body, but all he saw was the aqua-colored hospital gown and white surgical wrap.

He watched the woman pump a quarter-sized amount of sanitizer into her palms and rubbed her hands together. She headed for the door while speaking, "Don't move too much. You'll rupture your incisions and disband your stitches."

"What did I need stitches for?" Jhalil wondered and felt along his body with one of his hands.

"Your chest, eyebrow, and your leg."

"What happened to my leg?"

Slowly, the night's events came back to his remembrance. He remembered being hit in the head and feeling a sharp pain in his chest as Curt stomped it. But he couldn't recall what had happened with his leg.

"I really would have liked your doctor to explain this to you, but it's clear you have no idea what happened."

He simply blinked, dreading her next words.

"It appears someone kicked and broke your shin in three different places. Fortunately, no main arteries were severed, and doctors were able to save your leg. You'll definitely have to have therapy, Mr. Harrison, but it's touch and go if you'll be able to even use that leg again," she spoke softly and with sincerity. "I'm so, so sorry."

Jhalil's heart dropped. He could feel his eyes become watery at the thought of losing mobility in his leg. He grew emotional because there was no reason for him to be sitting here now, at the expense of the love of his life's mistakes.

"I'll give you a minute. But you do have a visitor if you're up for it. She says she's your fiancée. She drove behind the ambulance that brought you."

Jhalil shook his head and ignored the woman's words. More than anything, he could not figure out why Curt always tried so hard to take him back to the old Jhalil—the one who had no heart and who was once as ruthless as they came. He had God on his side, but God Himself would have to stop him from putting a hurting on Curt. As soon as he was up and walking again, he vowed to get his sweet, sweet revenge. As for Lorraina? He had no words for her right now. After all, she was the root of all this mess.

"Tell her to go home and don't ever come back here."

The nurse reluctantly nodded and left out. "Oh! Okay. Right away, sir."

As the door closed behind her, he broke down crying as he tried to imagine life without the use of one leg.

Chapter Twenty-Eight

"Mr. Harrison would rather not have company at this time," the nurse explained as gently as possible to Lorraina.

"What do you mean? I'm sure he would want to see me," she protested and stood up. "Did you tell him who I was?"

Her legs had begun to cramp up and she was tired, but she was determined to stay for as long as she could, if it meant supporting him through his recovery. Lorraina looked at the nurse who appeared uncomfortable and unsure about her request.

"I told him his fiancée was here and those were my instructions...to tell you to leave," she said with her head lowered.

She turned to walk away and Lorraina stared at the woman's back in confusion and slight anger. Who did this woman think she was? There was no way that Jhalil had given her such ridiculous orders. He was probably excited to see her and wanted a familiar face after such an eventful night. Lorraina ignored the nurse's protests and brushed past her.

"Ma'am, you cannot go back there! MA'AM!" the nurse called out while the secretary paged for security. The uniformed men came quicker than expected and Lorraina soon found herself being hoisted into a pair of muscular arms and physically carried out of the hospital.

"Don't make me call the police," one of the men threatened and stood in place until Lorraina turned around and headed to her car.

She was hurt, furious, and offended—why was the staff making it so hard to check up on her man? Had Jhalil really said that after all? Lorraina could not figure it out, so she decided to call it a night. She would go home and come back tomorrow when the staff changed. She cleaned up the mess of Curt's staged invasion and buried herself under the sheets until sleep claimed her.

The next morning, she did exactly what she planned. She went to the hospital, signed in under a different name, and marched into his room. She was prepared to throw a tantrum or two if anyone said anything. But surprisingly, there was no one in sight to protest her presence. As she rounded the corner and pulled back the curtain, she was puzzled to see a woman's backside facing her. This woman was not a nurse because she did not have any scrubs on. She wore jeans that were too tight, a T-shirt that rode up her midriff, and a simple ponytail.

From the build, Lorraina already knew who it was. It was someone she never thought she would run into ever again, especially in the company of Jhalil. It was his ex, Y'landa, and she looked absolutely beautiful even with her casual clothes on. Why was she here, and leaning over his bed? Why was she helping to feed him mashed potatoes, and wiping his face? Lorraina had so many questions.

"Ahem." She cleared her throat loudly.

Y'landa whipped around and looked surprised to see someone else in the room. "Hi, can I help you?"

"You can help me understand why you're here with my man, doing my job?"

"Obviously, if you were on your job, he wouldn't be here in the hospital."

"Ladies…that's enough," Jhalil said weakly and attempted to sit up on his own. "Lorraina, I thought I made it clear that I didn't want you here?"

"And *I* thought I made it clear that I'm not the enemy here. Please…just give me 10 minutes to explain everything that I know." She stared at him with sincerity, taking in his withdrawn appearance, and silently willing him to give her a chance.

"Y'landa, go down to the cafeteria for a second. Lorraina, come in and pull the curtain back. We need to talk."

Lorraina did as told and sat on the edge of the bed while Y'landa snatched up her purse from the windowsill and walked out. Jhalil looked better than what she imagined, especially because the last time she saw him, blood was everywhere. Still, she cringed at his bruises, bandages, and stitches, and felt guiltier at Y'landa's words. She was not totally responsible for Curt's actions, but she had literally slept with the enemy, so it made things just as bad.

"So, what's up, Jhalil? You're runnin' back to her now? What is this?"

Jhalil nonchalantly glanced at her and the fire in his eyes made her stop in her tracks. He stared her down coldly for several long moments, and then looked at the muted television screen.

"You have no room to talk or say anything. Thank you for calling for help that night—but that's as far as my kindness will go today."

Lorraina swallowed hard. "Baby…"

He held up his hand. "Y'landa was the one who showed me that video online of you dancing and allowing those men to do those things to you. Not only that, but Curt played a recording of you two making love and talking, and you said you wanted him to hurt me. Over what, Lorraina? I was nothing but good to you! How could you do me like that? I could've died that night, and God only knows if I'll be ever to use my leg again. It's all your fault," he accused.

She pointed her finger at him. "Don't do that to me...don't you DARE say that to me. I was tricked and assaulted!"

"So was I! The only difference is, you had a choice to stop it before it happened. You didn't have to run to Curt. You didn't have to leave me. You CHOSE to take his word over mine and got yourself in that situation. Look at you! You've changed and it's not in a good way!"

"He had EVIDENCE that you could possibly be..."

"*Evidence?*" Jhalil licked his parched lips and laughed bitterly. "The man doesn't even have a badge, Lorraina! How stupid can you be? That man lied to you! He's a con artist, and he didn't take well to your rejection or me standing up for you, so he did what he had to do, and he got what he wanted. He got you in the bed *again*, and he almost killed me. He knew that if he got in your mind, he could strike me next."

Lorraina stepped back, sensing the venom in his words.

"Now, I can't use one of my legs, and I can't go forth in my ministry, or lead my life normally from this day forward. You can hang it up on marriage or even a relationship. How can I marry somebody like you? There isn't a faithful bone in your body!"

Lorraina could cry. She sat there, numb to it all. "So, you're throwing our relationship away?"

"LISTEN TO YOURSELF! Didn't you do the same thing? I would have taken you back and forgiven you off the strength of knowing that you were blindsided. But you slept with him. That wasn't a mistake. You made a choice to cheat and that is what I cannot accept. Not only that, but your actions took Noah away. I loved that little boy and planned to adopt him! You should have just come to me. If you loved me, you should have fought for us and gotten to the bottom of it, instead of taking some psycho's word over mine." His voice was growing hoarser from raising it. He sat back in his bed and sighed. He looked worn out.

Lorraina was fully crying now. Jhalil had quickly become her life. Other than God, she lived for him. She did not know what she would do without him, and the thought killed her as she pleaded for him to take her back. He explained that Y'landa was helping him through the remainder of his recovery, and how he wished he had never left her in the first place. He told Lorraina that she had been nothing but trouble since day one, and he should have stayed away. He ordered for her to leave and to never contact him ever again. Lorraina felt dead inside. She literally had no one, and her and her promiscuous ways had caused her own destruction.

That night, as she popped a melatonin vitamin that would help her go to sleep, she settled in a warm bath and contemplated life. She thought about how gullible she had been when it came to men. She thought about how careless she had been when it came to her body. She even thought about her childhood and how her curiosity with sex was first piqued.

There was a man in her neighborhood—named Eugene—who all the kids loved and trusted. He was the ice cream man, and he would often give leftover treats to the children. He was in his early

20s, and to Lorraina, he was as tall as the trees in her grandmother's backyard. All the girls thought he was cute because of his smooth, cinnamon-colored skin, and deep, green eyes that would turn hazel in the fall. He seemed to take a liking to Lorraina especially. She always received two treats while the other children only received one.

It was on a really hot day in August that she finally got to tour his ice cream truck. To her surprise, he only allowed her to board the truck while her friends ran off in tears of disappointment. She was shown all his fine equipment and then given a cherry-flavored Popsicle. As she licked its contents, she noticed how his eyes widened and how he shifted in his seat. She blushed under the gaze of his eyes and continued to suck on her treat.

"Can I show you one last thing?" he questioned her.

"Mmhmm," she mumbled with her lips still stretched around the cold treat.

Eugene unzipped his pants right then and there and both Lorraina's treat and jaw dropped at the sight of his exposed flesh. She began to cry with terror and headed for the door. Her Popsicle fell to the ground and splattered all over her blue jeans. Her grandmother had always taught her right from wrong, and this was definitely wrong, even coming from Eugene.

"Where are you going?" he asked in panic.

"HOME! I'm tellin'!" she cried out and could not seem to shake the images of Eugene's body part. As she ignored his pleas to keep it a secret, she raced home, and the picture of his manhood stayed with her for the rest of her life.

A single tear fell down Lorraina's face now, as she realized she had always been curious about intercourse and the opposite sex from that moment on. There was nothing she could do to stop it, cure it, or make sense of it. No prayer, no counseling, and no girl talk could truly satisfy her appetite when it came to love making.

She wondered if something was wrong with her. She never admitted it to anyone, but she also had been touched a couple times on the school bus as a fifth grader. She had been touched in college by a professor, and in the workplace by a supervisor. It was like she was a magnet for assault—but why? What was so special about her?

She loved sex—*that*, she could confess. She loved the idea of creating music and magic with her body. She loved the thought that others craved what was between her legs. It was always something that gave her confidence, assurance, and validation as a woman. No matter how much women like her were looked down upon, she enjoyed the attention and the looks. But it wasn't healthy. As a woman of God, she should have a completely different mindset, but it was hard to do when sex was all you knew.

Sadness crept into her heart. Her addiction had been costly. Even now, as her hands touched her body, she thought of Jhalil and knew his intimacy would be something she missed more than anything. She grew sick at the thought that he would no longer frequent her body.

"God, please," she whispered as she began to drift off to sleep in the bathtub. "If you do nothing else for me, I thank You. But please deliver me from my illness. Please take away my addiction."

Chapter Twenty-Nine

It was the very next week that God honored Lorraina's prayer request. She was absently watching a soap opera when a commercial took over the television screen and encouraged viewers suffering from addictions to call the listed hotline. She scribbled the number down, reached for her cell phone, and took a deep breath. She dialed the numbers shakily, and then waited.

No one answered.

She decided to leave a message for the extension. She whispered as though she was in a room full of people, but really, it was only Lorraina standing in the middle of her kitchen. That is how ashamed she felt.

"Hi, I would like to remain anonymous at the moment, but I, um…I was calling because…because I have an addiction. I am addicted to sex. It has taken control of my life even though I've been in classes before, and I've received help before. Obviously, it didn't work," she laughed but there was no humor in it. "It's ruined relationships for me. It's clouded my judgment time and time again, and I'm sick of it. Please call me back at this number when you have a moment. Thank you so much."

Lorraina ended the call and sighed. Whatever happened would happen. She could not be concerned with anything else except getting better with each day. Since Jhalil had exed her out of his life, she had not eaten like she should, and the weight was just falling off her body. Her hair had not been done in days. She had only prayed a few times, and she had completely stopped attending church.

Her life was literally in shambles, and she knew God was not pleased with her.

As she prepared for bed that night, she received a call from an unknown number. Something in the pit of her stomach encouraged her to answer so she did.

"Hello?"

"Hi, my name is Dr. Rich Munn. My secretary forwarded me your number and message earlier, but I didn't get a name. I know it's late and inappropriate, but I could not help but to relate to your addiction. I, myself, could not live without sex or intimacy and it cost me my marriage, family, and six-figure salary. I had to reach out to you right away. Do you have time to talk more?"

"Um," Lorraina thought aloud and looked at the clock. "It is eight o'clock in the evening, however, I was only about to shower. I can talk, yes."

"What's your name?"

"Rain," she fibbed.

"Rain? Like the—"

"Yes, like the weather. Rain."

"Excellent. Call me Rich." There was some rustling in the background, and she assumed he was grabbing a pen and some paper. "This is my cell number, which you can keep. However, tomorrow and beyond, I'll always call you from my office, or meet with you in person. Is that doable?"

She nodded as though he could see her. "Yes, that's fine."

"Excellent," he spoke, and his voice softened. "Now tell me what's on your mind? Besides dealing with your addiction, *why* did you decide that you needed professional help? Please

241

keep in mind, this consultation and conversation is completely free."

Lorraina took a deep breath and figured it was now or never. No matter how it made her look, she would have to be honest in order to get honest results. She told him everything; she revealed most of her dealings with sexual intercourse or sexual contact, from her childhood to her adolescence and college years, to her adulthood. She told him about the men she had been with. She told him about the men she loved and those she only dated in order to satisfy her *craving*. She told him how she had messed up marriages and relationships, and how she was also a former pastor who encouraged others to flee from sin, but she could not even do the same. She told him about Jhalil and Curt, and their most recent fallout. She told him all her deepest secrets.

Rich listened on the other end with a judgment-free ear, scribbled on his notepad, and suggested that they meet for dinner tomorrow night. She agreed and went to bed with a much emptier heart and conscience. The following evening, she met him outside of his office building, which was adjacent to a Chinese restaurant. She was not big on this type of food, but she agreed because she needed the help.

"After you," he said and stepped to the side so she could enter the restaurant first. "Have you ever been here before?"

She sat down in the chair that he had pulled out for her. "I have not."

"They have excellent food," he pointed out and unbuttoned his suit jacket.

"Is 'excellent' your favorite word?" she joked.

"Oh, goodness. I've been told I say that too much."

"Just a little." Lorraina smiled.

They made small talk over an appetizer and just as their entrees were coming out, Lorraina noticed a couple coming in from the wheelchair-accessible ramp. She smiled compassionately, and thanked God for her legs. She turned back to Rich, who had asked her a question.

"I take that as a 'no'?" he questioned.

"What did you say?"

"I asked if you've contacted your fiancé since your last run-in?"

"Oh." Lorraina shook her head. "No. He's probably moved on, as I should. We haven't spoken at all."

"If you never heard from him again, how would that make you feel?"

Lorraina often thought of that question and sighed. In fact, she had just sent him an 'I love you' text this morning, but of course, he had not responded. Her eyes glazed over with tears.

"It would hurt me to the core. But I have to accept the consequences of my actions. I was wrong, and my actions caused him to get hurt."

Rich nodded and looked down at his plate. "Sort of like when my wife and I split. We aren't divorced, just separated. But I realized that I was toxic for her, and that I was willing to separate myself so that *she* could be free. Imagine that—a psychologist who couldn't even save his family. At the time I didn't know God, but now I do, and He's kept me since then. I miss her so much, and she won't let me see our kids, but I wouldn't want to interrupt her life again unless God tells me to go back."

"That's so real, Rich," she whispered. "I'm sorry to hear that."

"I'm man enough to accept my mistakes and consequences, as you said." He shrugged.

Lorraina bit into a piece of orange chicken and looked up when the waiter at the next table dropped a glass cup. He was standing before the man in the wheelchair and apologized. She squinted and eyed the man closer. No, it couldn't be. Of all places to be, she was in the same restaurant and breathing the same precious air as...*Jhalil?*

This was such a coincidence.

"Oh, my goodness," Lorraina said and dropped her head. "You see that guy in the wheelchair?"

"Yeah."

"That's my..." As she spoke, Rich cut off her words.

"Wait a minute." He stood up. "*Y'landa?*" His voice was loud and overpowered the soft music playing overhead.

Y'landa was accompanying Jhalil tonight and they both looked exhausted from the long week. She was helping to feed and tend to him, while he sat immobile and quiet. The two turned towards Rich and Lorraina, and Y'landa's eyes grew big especially.

"What are you doing here?" she asked him.

"You have no right to question me! What are you doing here, and with HIM?"

Jhalil spoke up this time and looked at Lorraina with bitterness. "You literally sent me a text eight hours ago, but you're here with another man? Is this another one of your flings, Lorraina? It doesn't take you long to bounce from the next one, huh? Unbelievable."

Lorraina removed the linen napkin from her lap and stood up. "He's helping me get better! He's a psychiatrist."

Rich looked over in confusion. "How do you two know each other?"

"That's Jhalil—the man I've been talking to you about."

"Woooow," Rich whistled and looked around. "So, we all are just one big happy family right now, huh? Where are the kids, Y'landa?"

"Wait, so who is she to YOU?" Lorraina wondered.

"My wife," he clarified. "The one I was telling you about."

"*Estranged* wife," she corrected. "You've been runnin' your mouth to her about me?"

"It doesn't matter. We're still married, and you have no right to keep my kids from me!"

"*Kids? Wife?*" Jhalil repeated and looked over at Y'landa in shock. "We've been on and off all this time, and you haven't told me anything about you being married with children. What the heck, Y'landa?"

"Let me explain!" she cried.

Jhalil wheeled himself away, while Rich dragged Y'landa outside and proceeded to scream at her. Lorraina sat back down at her seat and held her head in her hands. She had a headache forming.

Rich returned a few minutes later, seething, and trying to calm himself down. "I'm so sorry you had to be a part of that."

"It's fine. My life is one big ball of drama. I'm used to it."

"We can still talk if you'd like. I just don't know about that girl. I—I just don't know how I got to be so lucky with an idiot like that for a wife," he spewed, and she knew it was only the anger talking. After all, he had just professed and expressed his love to her, and now he was insulting her. "Are we done here?"

"We're done."

That was literally the last time she would ever see Rich again.

Chapter Thirty

It was now an entire month after the blowup at the restaurant, and Lorraina had not heard from Jhalil since. She knew he was on to better things, and she had no reason not to be as well. She picked up the pieces to what her life had become and asked God to put those pieces back together again. Little by little, she learned to live without him. She learned to live without a man period. She also recognized and learned self-love and wished she could show her younger self a thing or two.

She sought after another psychologist. This new doctor was a well-seasoned woman named Princess Waters. They met three times a week in her downtown office, and sometimes outside of their sessions. They became close and she was there for Lorraina like no one ever had been. In fact, they had just left a shopping center, and were heading their separate ways. Lorraina busied herself with a part-time secretary position at Princess's office and was now attending another church home.

Life was beginning to *finally* look up.

After she drove back to her cozy one-bedroom, one-bath apartment, she turned on the news and was alarmed to see Curt's face all over the news. He was wanted for murder by the FBI, and he was said to be armed and on the loose. She listened to the young news anchor's report.

"We spoke to the federal agents today, and here's what they know so far," the woman announced before the screen flashed *BREAKING NEWS* across it.

The image of a detective appeared on the screen at a press conference that was held earlier. He spoke with a lisp, "Mr. Randall is charming and intelligent, but he's extremely dangerous. He not only has organized several bank robberies, but he's played a major role in the murder of 29-year-old, Chelsea McCullen. McCullen is his ex-wife and the mother of his six children. We have reason to believe that he is seeking revenge on any and every woman he has ever been romantically involved with, according to a letter recently found in Randall's Northside home. He is not working alone either. We have sufficient evidence that he has been working with former FBI agents, Emilio Chavez and Julio Lechuga, to commit these crimes. Randall was recently charged in the beating of local pastor and community activist, Jhalil Harrison. We are warning all civilians to be on the lookout for this dangerous, dangerous man."

Lorraina felt sick to her stomach as she tried to comprehend what she had just heard and seen. He had truly fooled her with his gentleman act, and obviously, she wasn't the only one tricked and hurt by him. Six kids? This man had lost his mind. She felt sad about his ex-wife's death but was also grateful to God for covering and protecting her while in the presence of Curt because he could have done anything to her. She turned off the television and immediately called Jhalil. Surprisingly, he answered on the first ring.

"Jhalil, listen…"

He cut her off with his monotonous tone. "Yes, Lorraina. I've heard about Curt. A detective called me today and explained everything to me. Yes, this situation can't get any crazier. Yes, the thing with Y'landa was a surprise, and I guess it's karma for all the nasty things I said to you. Yes, I hate you and want nothing more than for you to never talk to me again."

She remained quiet, gripping her cell phone as if her life depended on it. She was relieved to hear his voice but was saddened by his harsh, unapologetic words.

He continued, and his voice grew softer, "But I'm also glad you didn't end up like his ex-wife, dead, and just a memory. I would have lost my mind knowing that something happened to you, and I did nothing to stop it."

She smiled in relief and felt a fresh wave of tears threatening to fall from her eyes. Unlike all the crying she had done lately, these were tears of joy.

"I know everything, Rain," he added. "And I'm sorry."

"We both did some crazy things. Do you forgive *me*?" she pondered.

"I do," he whispered back.

"Do you believe me when I say I had no idea or no say so in his attacks and plans, and that I never wanted to hurt you?"

"I do believe you."

Hesitantly, she asked the number one question on her mind. "Do you still love me?"

"I love you," he spoke without reluctance. "I never stopped."

That was truly music to her ears.

"But none of it matters anymore," he said. "My life, as I know it, is all over."

"Why do you say that? Your life isn't over. Your life's just beginning. Don't let this define your future. God isn't done with you yet."

"I'm honestly tired of hearing all of that," he admitted, and she could hear wind in the background. He must have been outside, enjoying the breeze. "I'm tired of it all. Maybe this is a dream that I haven't woken up from."

"Why are you talkin' like that? Where are you anyway?"

Jhalil sighed and there was great emotion in his response. "I just had to get away. I'm near Johnson's Pier."

"Johnson's Pier?" she repeated. "Why are you there? Who took you out there?"

"I caught an Uber. I just needed to clear my mind, you know?"

Her eyes narrowed in concern. "Be careful. That's one of the most dangerous places in the city. So many people fall in the river and drown every year," she said.

He laughed in her ear and the sound was forced and filled with agony. "Look at you. You're still lookin' out for me even after all the terrible things I've said to you."

"Who cares? We hurt EACH OTHER. None of that matters. Your happiness and peace of mind is all I care about."

"You really mean that?"

"Of course."

"Well, I'm afraid all that's over now. Just imagine how powerful we could have been as a couple really after God," he mused quietly and sniffed. "Demons would tremble at our power…and people would be amazed at our testimonies."

"And they still can," she said.

"I'm afraid that's all over, love. I've failed God way too much."

"Don't say that! For as long as you have breath in your body, you are forgiven and can make it right! It doesn't matter what we've done or what happened in our pasts; God's grace is sufficient. You told me that same thing. Remember?"

"I do, but I can't travel like I used to. I can't walk around freely and do what I need to do to preach the gospel. Our church has fallen apart. Our secrets are out. Who's going to join under my leadership? Not only that, but my leg is a vital part of my life and ministry."

Lorraina gripped the phone tighter against her ear. "I understand that, but baby…"

"There's nothin' you can say right now. I'm sorry. This is just too much for me," he said in between a hearty cry.

"Why do you keep talking like this? What's really going on?" she questioned. "Jhalil, talk to me. Where's your head at, baby?"

She didn't like how he sounded. She was sure that he was falling apart on the phone right then and there with her, and she feared for what may come. She headed for Johnson's Pier, which was a popular tourist spot. It was gorgeous but deadly, and had huge boulders overlooking the aggressive river. Many times, people would climb on the rocks to get a good selfie in, and then would fall to their death. She hoped that was not in his plans as she headed for the door without shoes or a jacket on.

"My legs." He was openly crying now. "It turns out, not only was the right one shattered, but it's been infected since the surgery, and it spread to my other leg. They may have to amputate both legs. What am I going to do without my legs, Lorraina?"

"God can do ALL things and you know that! We've got to speak healing, Jhalil!"

"I GIVE UP! You can have this life!" he yelled.

Lorraina encouraged him to stay on the line and drove as fast as she possibly could without getting a speeding ticket or getting into an accident. She prayed for his mind and for God to protect him until she arrived. She searched through the grasslands and stumbled over wood chunks and tree stumps that had decayed.

She finally saw Jhalil's silhouette as he stood on the edge of a boulder and looked down into the never-ending water. The currents were strong and brash. His crutches were tossed to the side of him. His legs were shaky and unsteady, and the only thing keeping him upright was the powerful wind that literally seemed to hold him up.

Lorraina kept her movements slow and purposeful and walked up to him with caution. She chose not to say anything until she was right behind him. Just as he dropped his phone into the water and began to fall forward, Lorraina reached out and grabbed him. Jhalil had lost quite a few pounds since his incident, but he still had a lot of weight on him, and especially his semi-paralyzed legs.

She held onto him and backed away from the edge of the boulder with unexpected supernatural strength. There was no way she could have ever pulled his bodyweight, let alone her own. He was crying and looked helpless as she pulled him to safety. She thanked God that she made it in time and hugged his body to hers.

"Baby, don't you ever leave me! You hear me? I would have died without you!" she declared.

"I'm sorry. God, I'm so sorry. I'm sorry," is all he kept repeating.

They sat there for hours, crying, hugging, praying, and rocking back and forth in the cool breeze. Eventually, Lorraina called for help, and she continued to nestle against him as they waited.

"How did we get so broken?" he asked her and looked off into the distance. Tearstains coated his cheeks. "How did we each reach our breaking points like that?"

"I don't know. But only God can put us back together again," she whispered in his ear. "This time let's allow God to *really* heal us. I don't want to waste any more of my life on the wrong people, and on the wrong things."

He closed his eyes with a smile of agreement.

Epilogue

(Five years later…)

"Joshua Hardison," the dean called out over the roars of cheers and claps.

The auditorium was packed, wall to wall, with people as family members, faculty, and graduates all gathered for the long-awaited commencement ceremony. Lorraina stood off to the side of the stage, knowing she was going to be called shortly, and attempted to calm down some. She was half nervous and half excited at her accomplishments.

In just four years, she had completed her second Bachelor's degree in psychology, with a concentration in family therapy. God had blown her mind and taken her down a path she never expected.

Not only had she gone back to school, but she had been blessed to open her own office building that focused on saving women, saving children, and saving families. It was filled with the best of the city's therapists and counselors, and she was thrilled to be jumping in headfirst to the role just as soon as she accepted this certificate. With her new credentials, she would be able to counsel women affected by sexual and domestic abuse and give treatment to women who were addicted to sex. She knew her grandmother would be so proud of her.

Her eyes skimmed the crowd while she embarked on the impossible task of finding her loved ones. *Bingo.* She should have known that her husband would make some gaudy, larger-than-life sign to draw her attention. Throughout this journey, he had been so supportive and helpful when it came to the late nights of studying and preparing for her courses. Jhalil was just as excited as she was, and for that, she loved him.

Upon being delivered from her sexual addiction, and thoroughly receiving the help and counseling that she needed, Lorraina accepted his proposal, and it was one of the greatest decisions she ever made. They were going almost four years strong now and were unstoppable. God had renewed their minds and ordered their steps to present one of the most effective marriage ministries to the city.

They were no longer heading a church as pastors, but they were elders at their church home. They had even signed with the premier publishing company called Anointed Ink Publications and had written a best-selling book about marriage and ministry. To date, six marriages had been saved under their leadership. Life was beautiful and Lorraina knew it was all because they had *fully* accepted God's Will for their lives instead of orchestrating in the flesh.

She waved and blew a kiss to Jhalil, and then tuned back into the older gentleman who was calling out names and awarding the graduates with handshakes. It was time.

"Lorraina Harrison," he called and looked at her with a smile.

Lorraina could hear her family rooting for her, although the dean had warned everyone to keep quiet until the end. She took a deep breath and took a few steps forward in her pumps, and then raised both her index fingers. She looked to the Heavens and continued to point upward as she whispered, "It was all You, God."

She accepted her degree, posed for a photo, and then retreated to her seat. There were close to 80 more graduates that had to be called, so she ducked low, and tiptoed out of the arena. She looked for the landmark where her husband told her to meet him. As she rounded the corner, there were balloons blowing in the breeze and a small crowd of smiling faces that greeted her. Her eyes widened in shock because she had no idea so many people were present for her special day.

"Congratulations!" everyone yelled in unison, and she ran into the arms of her family, kissing them one by one on the cheek. She hugged Khloey, Princess, Jhalil, her pastor and first lady, a few church members, and the people who gave her even more reason to live, her children.

There was Noah, Jhalil Junior, and Jada. After more than a year of searching, they had been reunited with Noah and were awarded full custody and guardianship of him after explaining to his family what had happened. Noah was now six, Jhalil Junior was two, and Jada was seven months. They were both seated in a stroller and looking up at their mother with bright smiles. Although she had carried them both for nine months, had a C-section with Junior, and had faithfully juggled motherhood with all her other responsibilities, she could not believe that they both looked identical to their father.

She chuckled at the thought and looked at her husband. Jhalil was fine as ever in his navy blue button-down shirt. He had only buttoned it beginning at his navel, so his muscular, tattooed chest was showing. He wore white cargo shorts, and navy blue loafers, and had a pair of tan shades propped on top of his bald head. Yes, her man had completely shaved his hair off, and he looked good enough to eat. The older he got, the wiser, more confident, and finer he seemed to get as well. Sexiness oozed from him even now as he licked his lips and grabbed Jada from the stroller. Jhalil noticed her watching him, so he winked.

Despite what doctors said, he was still walking, dancing and running on his God-given legs. He had been completely healed and fortunately, there was no lasting damage to his limbs. She often found herself praising God for him and their journey through hell and back. He was all hers for a lifetime and beyond. She was especially thankful for being able to deliver healthy, happy babies. She would not trade her family for anything else in the world.

It was like she was a new creature in Christ all over again, but *for real* this time. She did not plan on backsliding ever again, and she would forever tell the devil to get behind her if temptation ever arose. People like Capri, Curt, and whomever else from her past were long gone. In fact, the last she heard was that Capri moved out of town to start a new life, and Curt was locked away to rot in some prison. She felt good. She felt free. She *was* free.

Lorraina unzipped her black graduation gown and tucked it on top of the stroller. She kept her cap on and made sure her long tresses were still beautiful and vibrant beneath it. She wore a flowy cream-colored dress and opted to remain sleeveless because it was so humid out. Gold earrings and bangles, and gold high heels completed her attire.

"Where to now, baby?" Jhalil asked and led them to the corner of the intersection. They had parked in a structure not far from the arena. He leaned over to kiss her, and then placed his hand on the small of her back.

"I'm so glad y'all could make it," she told everyone and grabbed Jhalil's hand as they crossed the street. "I'm ready to eat!"

The End

ABOUT THE AUTHOR

Olivia Shaw-Reel has written nearly 30 books before her 30th birthday. Her award-winning novels, *Soul Cry, What God Has Joined Together, and Matters of the Hart: A Tale of the Dysfunctional Hart Sisters*, have become her biggest-selling books to date.

She also hosts *The Reel Love Podcast* with her husband, Paris. Olivia lives in Milwaukee, WI.

Visit the official storefront for updates and to purchase autographed paperbacks at ***osrbooks.com***.

Follow her on Instagram, TikTok and Facebook at ***@oliviashawreel***.

Please also spread the word by completing a book review on Amazon or Goodreads! Olivia loves hearing feedback on her work!

OTHER TITLES FROM THE AUTHOR

Soul Cry, Vol. 3
What God Has Joined Together, *2-Book Series*
Baptized in Her Seduction: A Church Love Affair,
2-Book Series
Lord, Save Me From Myself, Vol. 2
Meet Me at the Altar
Full Court Mess
The Only Gift
Andrue & Sy'mone: An Urban Love Affair, *3-Book Series*
Can't Leave Him Alone After the Love We Made,
Book 1
Kiss Me @ Midnight
Stuck Wit'chu
Sins of a Mafia Princess
Matters of the Hart: A Tale of the Dysfunctional
Hart Sisters, *3-Book Series*
In Love With Everything You Could Be
Stalked by My Pastor, *Book 1*
A Christmas Miracle
Who's Loving You This Christmas?
Saved, Sanctified, & Filled With Anxiety
Compilation
When Mark Met Tammy: Love Letters to My
Parents

www.ingramcontent.com/pod-product-compliance
Lightning Source LLC
Chambersburg PA
CBHW070504030726
47503CB00004B/1156